What's

The

Point?

Cyberworld Publishing

www.cyberworldpublishing.com

Cyberworld Publishing
Jindalee St
Toronto, Australia

Books by Olivia Stowe

Charlotte Diamond Mystery Series
By The Howling

Retired With Prejudice

Coast to Coast

An Inconvenient Death

What's The Point?

White Orchid Found

The Savannah Series
Chatham Square

Savannah Time

Inspirational Christmas collections
Spirit of Christmas (2010)

Christmas Seconds (2011)

Other
Fiddler's Rest

What's The Point?

Charlotte Diamond Mysteries Five

Olivia Stowe

Chapter One: Journey Back into Chaos

All of the instincts of retired FBI senior investigator, Charlotte Diamond, started to jangle as she gazed out across the swirling departure gate crowd at Amsterdam's Schiphol international airport and her eyes settled on the figure of the young man lurking behind a column. What had arrested her attention was not so much what he was looking at but what he wasn't looking at. What he wasn't looking at was her very intimate friend, Brenda Boynton—known by most of those gawking at her as the top box-office movie star Brenda Brandon. Presently the silver-haired beauty, possibly more gorgeous in her late forties than she had been in her thirties, was struggling beside Charlotte, trying to gain control of the various boxes and bags she had accumulated in the duty-free stores. As she was doing so, she was attracting the surprised recognition and admiring attention of all of the men in the waiting area—except that one young man snuggling behind the column—and many of the women as well. The whole crowd had been set in motion by the announcement that the first class passenger boarding for the KLM flight from Schiphol to Baltimore's BWI airport could now commence.

From many years of experience, Charlotte's eyes traced to the focus of the young man's attention. A distinguished-looking older man, with a younger, blonde woman on his arm, had reached the gate, obviously ready to board. As Charlotte watched, the older man turned toward his companion, leaned his head down, and they kissed. The young woman then remained standing where she was as the older man handed over his ticket to the attendant at the gate. At the entrance into the tunnel to the plane, he turned, and the young woman blew him a kiss.

Charlotte looked back at the young man standing behind the pillar and could see that he was intently watching all of this.

"Are you coming, Charlotte? They've called our flight."

Charlotte's attention was taken away from the brief exercise of her detective instincts, during which a dozen scenarios were going through her head, by the rich contralto voice of the woman she so deeply loved. Charlotte was no different from millions of theatergoers. All Brenda had to do was speak something in that gorgeous voice of hers, tilt her silver-blonde-encased head slightly to one side, and smile that shy, disarming smile of hers and Charlotte melted.

"Umm, sorry, I was daydreaming," Charlotte said as she hefted her lumpy bulk out of the departure-lounge seat and stretched a good distance toward the ceiling, knowing that, first class or no first class, she'd feel cramped on the air journey home.

"Oh, so you weren't watching that young man watching the May-to-December couple?"

"You've been with me too long," Charlotte said, with a laugh.

"Never too long," Brenda answered, looking levelly at her companion. "Almost too late, but never too long." It was delivered like a classic line from an old wartime movie, and it made Charlotte glow and feel like she was the luckiest woman in the world.

Charlotte felt the inhibiting presence of several hundred people waiting to get on the Airbus A330-200. There was nothing she wanted to do at this moment so much as take Brenda in her arms and show her appreciation for the two having found each other.

"Wouldn't that just make the evening news," Charlotte muttered, grabbing for her carry-on bag to avoid the unnerving temptation to reach for something else.

"Beg pardon?" Brenda asked.

"Just that you're right. I was watching that young man. And look, there's what I expected to see."

The young woman who had just kissed away the older man had walked back out of the crowd now bunching up around the podium waiting for their call to board. The young man had come out from behind the column, and the two had almost collided in an embrace. It was an embrace that included a more-than-friendly kiss on the lips.

"Come on, Sherlock," Brenda said as she tugged on Charlotte's arm. "If we're going to make our call before they open the cattle gates, we have just enough time to thread our way through the gathering crowd."

"Let them go," Charlotte said, standing her ground. "I want to see what happens with that couple. How can they even be here if they aren't getting on the airplane? And, as for the crowd, they can't sit in our seats anyway. We'll be entombed in that flying canister for hours. I prefer to be on my feet as long as possible."

"Whatever you say, master." Brenda smiled one of her brilliant movie smiles, and Charlotte thought she could hear a sigh go around the waiting room, where, although people were bunching up around the gate to the plane, many of them were still staring back at Brenda, obviously recognizing and reveling in who she was. Charlotte was fairly certain that if they'd moved toward the gate now, a wide pathway would open up to let Brenda pass. There might even be some bowing and scraping.

Instead, they both watched the young couple move away from them along the corridor between the gates. The couple stopped and both looked up at a flight board.

"There's your answer," Brenda said. "They have another flight to go to."

"That's certainly brave timing. And such chutzpah."

"Well, we are in Europe, you know," Brenda said. And then she laughed that lilting laugh of hers, and Charlotte heard another sigh go around the room.

* * * *

"What are you thinking? You've been quiet for more than an hour."

"I'm surprised you noticed, as busy as you've been signing autographs."

"But aren't you glad I took the aisle seat?" Brenda asked, with another one of her signature laughs. "However, you're changing the subject. Of course I noticed you were quiet."

"That man."

"What man?"

"The prosperous-looking banker type who was seen off by the young woman—he's sitting just a couple of rows in front of us. I've been thinking about him. Don't you think we should say something to him about what we saw back at the airport?"

"I declare, Charlotte Diamond, that when you took the Myers-Briggs personality test, you must have maxed out on the 'Judgment' scale."

"Why, yes I did," Charlotte said, with a laugh. "That's pretty much required to get through the battery of tests to enter the FBI, you know."

"I can imagine. Well, I'm not going to tell him. What did we actually see?"

"Enough. Enough to put him on guard."

"Well, think about it for a while—but only off and on, please. Let's enjoy what we spent to be in first class—and let him enjoy it as well. If you want to do it, wait until we've arrived and are picking up the luggage. Why spoil what he paid to luxuriate in first class?"

"I suppose."

"What you need, Charlotte Diamond, is a vacation from all this sleuthing."

"We've just had a vacation. We've had two weeks on a river cruise ship on the Rhine, enjoying the Christmas markets."

"And what did you do on that cruise? You got yourself embroiled in a murder and a jewel theft."

"But . . ."

"I know. But you thoroughly enjoyed it."

"Yes, I guess I did. More after it was over, though."

"We should travel with your brother and sister more often. They're fun."

"Travel again with Chance and Marilyn? Why ever for? You know what I said about them . . . what always happens when they are around. And it did so on this cruise, didn't it?"

"Yes. As you said, murder and mystery follow them. But you thrive on mystery and murder. I do think you had the best vacation of all of us."

"Yes, perhaps I did, but I'm looking forward to some peace and quiet in Hopewell. How soon did you say we needed to be down in Florida for the movie shoot?"

"Two weeks, maybe three. I'll have to call Aaron when we get back home and find out if everything is still on schedule. And he said something about Tony and DeeDee coming for a week so Tony and I can do preliminary work with the movie script. I'm looking forward to some down time on the river too—even though January is usually my least favorite time on the Maryland Eastern Shore. I miss Sam and Rocket. I'll bet Sherry will be glad to see us back too. It's been virtually six weeks with the Hollywood shoot followed by this Rhine cruise."

"Yes, a couple of weeks with just the two of us and the dogs sounds divine."

"Divine? Did I hear you use the word 'divine'? I do think that you have been suborned to the world of the movies already. I would never have thought of a hardboiled FBI agent using a word like that."

"A much-retired FBI agent," Charlotte countered.

"Not that much. You're still up to your neck in intrigue. Even in the departure hall of Schiphol airport."

"Look at him up there," Brenda. "He looks like he doesn't have a care in the world. And yet he's living a world of lies and doesn't know it."

"Maybe," Brenda said. "And then again maybe he does know it and yet still enjoys whatever time he has with a young trophy wife. It's really quite European, you know. He might not be all that excited to hear from you on the subject of infidelity."

When they got to the baggage area at BWI airport in Baltimore, Maryland, Charlotte was glad she hadn't said anything and Brenda shot her an amused "I told you so" look.

As the baggage was arriving on the belts, a man in a chauffeur's uniform was directed to three expensive bags by the distinguished-looking older man who had farewelled the young woman at Schiphol airport, and then the older man was hugging and talking with a woman near his age, who was matronly, but very well taken care of—and who was swathed in a mink coat.

Brenda and Charlotte watched as the threesome trundled out to the curb, where a black limousine, its engine idling and a policeman guarding it rather than what he should have been doing—giving it a ticket—was waiting for them.

"So, what do you think?" Brenda asked.

"About what? About who he must be to be treated so royally?"

"No. About the young woman at Schiphol. Mistress or daughter?"

"Who cares? Either way, I was wrong and you were right. I've had enough of sleuthing for a while. If your Jag hasn't been stolen from the parking lot, let's cruise on up route 50 to the Choptank. I've had enough of mystery for a couple of weeks; I've obviously lost my edge."

"That would never happen, darling," Brenda said with a twinkle in her eye. "I'm sure there will be yet another mystery or two awaiting you when we get home."

* * * *

The drive home to the village of Hopewell on the Choptank in Brenda's mercifully unmolested Jaguar roadster led east of Baltimore to cross the Chesapeake Bay on Route 50. From there they turned east on 331 on the way down the east side of the Choptank River to their normally sleepy riverine village. The first thing they saw in their entrance into the village, however, was a noisy bulldozer. It was working in the center of the riverside lot just to the north of Brenda's eighteenth-century brick two-story mansion, which had once been the plantation house for the whole area.

"What in the . . . ? I thought that lot was yours, Brenda."

"It is. Or at least I thought so too. This must be some sort of mistake." Charlotte could tell that Brenda's voice was strained, that the sight of the bulldozer felling trees on the lot was very disturbing to her. "But I'll have to check. I admit that I haven't kept track of property rights here. I'll call my financial administrator, Frank Edmunds, straight away. Do you think we should go over there and—"

"Not much point in hassling the guy on the bulldozer," Charlotte answered. "He's not likely to know anything. We could ask him to stop until we got this checked out, but it looks like he's closing it down for the night anyway. Can't do any more harm before you have a chance to confirm your ownership. You go on in the house and call, and I'll go over and ask this guy who he works for."

"Vario Construction out of New York is all I know," the bulldozer operator answered when Charlotte approached him. "I'm subcontracted from over in Easton. They've called in a whole bunch of dozers. I don't know anything about a property dispute. But I'm shutting down for the night anyway."

"Several bulldozers? I only see the one," Charlotte said.

"Walk on up the street; you'll see a whole line of them. I've heard they're clearing this whole street out to the point. Sort of hope they don't plan on taking the brick house next door down, though."

"They can't. It's on the historical register," Charlotte said, "and there's no chance that the woman who owns it is going to sell it so it can be bulldozed down. I think someone's got it wrong. Maybe even in the wrong town. I have a house on this street too. And there certainly shouldn't be any bulldozing going on that I don't know about."

"Yeah, why?"

"Because I'm mayor of the town. No one's come to the town council with any redevelopment plans."

"Well, we've been working here for a week. Down the street, quite a bit has been done already. Maybe I should check in with my super before tomorrow morning."

"Yes, maybe you should do that. I've been gone for several weeks, so I have some checking to do too."

Charlotte marched back to Brenda's house. As she was mounting the stairs to the main door in the floor over the English basement, it hit her that the name Vario sounded familiar. She'd have to dig deep in her mind to figure out the connection, though. She found Brenda sitting in a chair in the kitchen by the telephone and looking stunned.

"Did you get hold of Frank Edmunds?"

"Yes. But at home. He says he'll have to go into the office to check the paper files . . . and he'll call me back."

"But does he remember—?"

"No. He says he doesn't remember anything about an extra parcel of land here in Hopewell on my property list. But he said it could just be that it's included in the plat for this house."

"I'm sure it must be, Brenda. You say your family has always owned this land, as far as you know? And you don't recall your father saying anything about selling that lot?"

"He couldn't have, surely. My mother was murdered and her body abandoned on that lot. My father would never have sold it. He didn't need the money. He'd never go on the land, but he told me more than once that he'd never let it be developed."

Brenda was hunched over, close to tears. Charlotte pulled a chair up close beside her, enveloped Brenda in her arms, and rocked her back and forth. "There, there. I'm sure it will all work out."

"And this house," Brenda said, almost as if she hadn't heard Charlotte, "It's full of dust. I don't think anyone's cleaned since we've been gone. I've got to call Edith and find out if she's been ill. The bulldozing must really have raised dust. I've never seen this place this dusty."

"Let's not think about any of that now," Charlotte cooed, thinking that Brenda must be in shock. Charlotte hadn't known her to care about some like a bit of dust in the house before. "It will all work its way out. It just must be a misunderstanding. In a bit, I'll go up to the Welles where Sherry Langdon's been keeping Sam and Rocket. And I'll bring them back. That will give us something else to think about until we get this sorted out."

"Yes, please do. Right away. I'll be OK. It's just such a shock. My mother . . ."

Brenda couldn't complete the sentence. When she was a young girl, her mother had been murdered and found in the reeds at the river edge shallows on that forested lot next door. For a while there even had been suspicion that Brenda herself had killed her—and she lived for decades under a cloud. This was largely what prompted her father to send her to Hollywood, where she had become a major motion picture star. It was only in the last year, when, under a cloud for the murder of the woman living with her in Hollywood, that Brenda had retreated back to her home village—and into the arms of Charlotte, recently retired there herself. It had been Charlotte who had discovered who had actually murdered Brenda's mother all those years ago—but not until after another body had been found on the riverbank on that lot. For that matter, Charlotte had also uncovered who had murdered the woman in Hollywood. Brenda had virtually clung to her heroine ever since.

As Charlotte left the house, she wondered what was happening with Edith Smith, Brenda's part-time cleaning lady. Edith was as weird as they came. She lived on a small farm, called the Clagett farm, just outside the village on the approach to River Street and was very much the recluse. She was prone to wearing plain cotton frocks and muddy combat boots—except in the house—and could be seen skittering aimlessly around the village in the shadows like a frightened rabbit.

Charlotte was still thinking on this as she walked up River Street toward the point, which ended in a large piece of property walled off at the end of River Street. It belonged to a former CIA counterintelligence

17

chief who Charlotte had known and who had disappeared to great fanfare and a full-scale, but trumped-up investigation. Charlotte had seen him more recently when she was in Hollywood with Brenda, though, and had discovered that his disappearance had been manufactured as some sort of international spy operation cover-up that Charlotte didn't even want to begin to try to figure out.

The first thing she saw when she looked up from her introspection was the line of large bulldozers the construction worker had said were there. They were lined up near the end of River Street toward the point and on the side of the road that Charlotte's own cottage was located—on the river side. The second thing she noticed, what set her heart racing and started her running in a waddling gait up the street on her chubby legs, was that the house beyond hers was a flattened pile of timbers and roofing. It had been bulldozed to the ground.

That was the Wellses' house—the house of a couple that had been on an archeology dig for most of the time Charlotte had lived in Hopewell. It was the house that the schoolteacher, Sherry Landon, who was taking care of Charlotte and Brenda's Siberian husky, Sam, and Rocket, their boxer, was renting.

Her eyes hadn't deceived her. The house had been demolished, as had two of the houses across the street. There was no sign of Sherry or the dogs.

Confused and in shock, Charlotte went back to her own house, next door to the demolished house. She entered, struggling with the lock on the front door until she discovered with dismay that it wasn't locked; stumbled into the living room; and sat heavily down on the sofa. She had to think. It was all such a great shock.

As she calmed down, she began to look around and her concern deepened. This wasn't the way she'd left the room. Some small items had been moved around. Even the recliner and TV had been moved. She rose from the sofa and walked from room to room in the cottage. It wasn't just that items had been moved. There were signs of habitation— continued habitation. There was food in the refrigerator, dishes in the sink, dirty laundry in the basket on top of the washer, and both men's and women's clothing that wasn't hers hanging in the master bedroom closet. The bed wasn't even made up as she had left it. She had no idea what this was all about, but she'd find out. But not until she'd gotten Brenda's problems sorted out. Brenda came first. And at least her house was still standing. Regardless, she was sick with worry about where Sherry and the dogs were—and if they were safe.

When she returned to Brenda's house, she found her companion in even deeper frustration than she'd left her. Charlotte held off on telling her about the bulldozed houses and the missing dogs.

"Has Edmunds called back?" Charlotte asked?

"Yes. He found papers showing that my father sold the lot to someone named Rizo back in the early 1970s. Dad never said anything to me about it, Charlotte. I don't know what's happening. I never would have thought that Dad would—"

"We'll sort it all out tomorrow, Brenda. You need to get to bed now. You've just flown across the Atlantic to be dropped in the middle of a shock."

"Dad would never—"

"Up you come. Upstairs. I'll draw a bath. After than it's straight to bed."

"Sam and Rocket."

19

"Tomorrow. We'll get them tomorrow. Tonight you need your full rest." Charlotte wasn't about to load Brenda down with what Charlotte had and hadn't found up River Street. Not tonight. She'd have to broach this carefully and in stages. Tomorrow Charlotte would be up before Brenda and would start canvassing the neighborhood on what was happening. The Vales, who ran the B&B, the Hopewell House Inn, across the street, would know. Or Don Dunkel, the Episcopalian chaplain.

As they trudged up the stairs, with Charlotte supporting the suddenly diminished, no-longer-radiant movie star, Brenda whispered something.

"What was that, Brenda?"

"Edith Smith. Very strange. I called her, and she acted like she didn't even know me. She said she knew nothing about cleaning the house—she'd been doing it for months, though. It didn't even sound like her."

"We'll sort that out tomorrow too—or the day after. Edith's nothing if not strange. A dusty house is the least of our problems now. It's probably a blessing. Edith's obviously gone around the bend. We'll find another housekeeper. We probably need someone full time, anyway. To bed. A bath and to bed. No more thinking or worrying. We'll get it all fixed tomorrow."

Brenda sighed and snuggled closer to Charlotte. "I'm glad I found you, Charlotte Diamond."

"Not half as glad as I am," Charlotte answered. And she meant it. Nothing else mattered. None of this madness they'd come home to mattered. Not as long as they had each other.

But as far as coming home for a rest . . . Charlotte knew that just wasn't going to happen.

Chapter Two: All Fall Down

They'd only gone as far as the backyard of Charlotte's own cottage—to the Adirondack chairs overlooking her dock into the Choptank River—before Charlotte suggested that they sit. Her purpose had been to get Brenda away from the noise of the bulldozing in the woods next door to her house and the excuse was that the dogs needed exercise—and something to tire them out and calm them down from the exuberance of meeting up with their mistresses again. Charlotte would have suggested going even farther along the riverbank—if she herself wasn't winded—except that the noise of the bulldozer in the woods would only be replaced by construction noise coming from down on the point.

Brenda had been so distracted by the attentions of Sam and Rocket and dejected in her dismay over the destruction of the wooded lot that she had been looking down at the frozen ground under their feet or out toward the river the entire walk, which Charlotte took as a godsend. It meant that Brenda hadn't yet seen the collapsed Wells house one lot farther toward the point from Charlotte's cottage.

Brenda had fallen into an exhausted sleep as soon as Charlotte got her to bed the previous night and was still asleep when Charlotte woke up. Charlotte dressed and slipped out of the house, bound for Zenna's Russian Bakery across and down the street in the community center that had been made out of the long-disused village schoolhouse, where Charlotte picked up croissants, milk, and cream for their breakfast.

It was barely light when Charlotte came out of the bakery, where Zenna had greeted her like a long-lost auntie but had seemed as bewildered as Charlotte on what was happening on the previously quiet and sedate River Street. Charlotte was looking back up the street toward Brenda's house and then across the street from there to the Vale's B&B, where Charlotte planned to go after breakfast to find out from Todd Vale what was going on. She knew that his wife, Joyce, wouldn't speak to her because of old grudges, but Charlotte was the town's mayor and Todd was a city councilor, so it wasn't just idle curiosity that motivated Charlotte's interest or that would obligate Todd to talk to her.

As Charlotte looked up the street, though, her attention was arrested by a figure scuttling off around the side of the B&B and over toward Penn Street, which dead-ended into River. The figure was already at the side of the Episcopalian church before Charlotte realized from the loose cotton frock the woman was wearing, the combat boots, and the stringy hair that it was Edith Smith, Brenda's wayward cleaning lady. Charlotte made a mental note to drive out to Clagett's farm that afternoon to pin Edith down on her position with Brenda. She fully intended to give the woman notice and to find someone more suitable, permanent, and more fully employed to clean the mansion.

Charlotte had had no more than that moment for that thought, however, as she heard a horn honk, turned back toward River Street to locate the origin of the noise, and then only had time to brace herself for the onslaught of two very happy dogs. Sam and Rocket were home.

"I'm sorry I couldn't get in touch with you," Sherry said when Charlotte managed to convince the dogs to let her walk back up the street to where Sherry Landon was standing next to her car in front of Brenda's house. "I knew you'd be home today, and it all happened so fast. I was only given two days' notice to get out of the Wellses' house before they knocked it down. I didn't know what else to do but to take the dogs over to the house of a teacher who works with me."

"Do you need a place to stay?" Charlotte asked.

"No, my friend—Patty Wainwright; I think you've met her— lost her roommate and it's convenient for me to move in with her. No room for Sam and Rocket on a permanent basis, though."

"We couldn't be happier to have them back. What do you know about what's going on here? Why was the Wells house demolished?"

"I have no idea. It's all happened so fast, and everyone I talked to was being secretive about it all. They had already started doing something down on the point when I got notice to vacate. I didn't have a written lease to protect me, so I just packed up."

"And my cottage. It looks like someone has taken up residence there."

"Yes. I've seen a man and woman coming and going. But I didn't talk with them. I assumed you gave them permission to be there. Every time I saw the man leave the house he was going down to the point."

24

"Hmmm. I'll have to talk to the Realtor about that. I don't remember now what I told her she'd could do with the cottage. I know we talked about the possibility of renting it. But my things are still in it; I haven't moved out."

As Charlotte was saying this, she saw that activity had begun again on the lot next door, and she quickly concluded her discussion with Sherry, wanting to get back into the house and be by Brenda's side before the disturbing bulldozer work started up again.

Brenda was up and sitting by the phone, making calls, when Charlotte brought the breakfast croissants up to the kitchen from the basement.

"Frank Edmunds has worked through the night on this," Brenda reported. "He says he's found a bill of sale made out to a Sal Rizo for the lot but that there's evidence it's still registered to my father's estate—and thus to me—and that I've apparently been paying the taxes on it. He says he'll work with the county records today and drive over there tomorrow. I asked him if he can get the bulldozing stopped, but he didn't think he could."

"I'm so sorry, Brenda. But the dogs are down in the basement. Sherry's brought them back." Charlotte didn't mention that they hadn't been just down at the Wells house. "After breakfast, let's take them for a walk along the river."

Brenda hadn't been sure she'd be up to it, but the sound of the bulldozing started up while they were eating breakfast, and this decided Brenda in favor of the walk. "Anything not to have to listen to those trees going down," she'd said with a shudder.

After they'd been sitting in the chairs by Charlotte's dock for a while and staring out over what must be frigid waters of the Choptank

25

in early January and watching the dogs having a ball at being home again, Charlotte sensed that there was more on Brenda's mind than the bulldozing back by the old federal mansion.

"I talked to Tony this morning too," Brenda said in hesitant voice.

Tony Trice was the young movie heartthrob actor Brenda had done several films with. Charlotte, and Tony, were among the few who knew that Tony was Brenda's son by an early indiscretion before she'd gone into movies. Brenda, having seen from afar Tony's innate acting talent, had assured that he got a break in the movies. His relationship to Brenda, though, had only recently been revealed to Tony and Charlotte.

"Yes. How is he?"

"He's doing fine. He—and DeeDee Yance are coming here this week. It was Aaron's idea. He'll be in the movie down in Florida with me—and DeeDee might as well—and he's coming here so we can go over the script before we appear in Florida."

"Ahh," Charlotte said. But what she thought was that she probably knew what was bothering Brenda. Brenda liked to think that Tony didn't know that Brenda was attracted to women. She'd been living with the costume designer Helga Lund in Hollywood until Helga was murdered, but Brenda had a blind spot toward Tony knowing that was the case—or that there had been anything serious to their relationship. And now Brenda was living with Charlotte here in Hopewell. Of course Tony would know Brenda's preferences and living arrangements, Charlotte thought. But she didn't want to be the one to burst Brenda's bubble on this topic.

DeeDee Yance had played the ingénue role in Brenda's last film, and even Charlotte had been able to see that after a few days of

26

sparring and thinking they didn't like each other, that Tony and DeeDee obviously did like each other. Brenda, the doting, protective mother, albeit from afar by necessity, had walked on eggs with DeeDee since then. It was clear that Brenda wasn't wild about DeeDee—Charlotte downright thought the young woman was a shallow, spoiled brat—and Brenda was at a loss how to relate to her. DeeDee, of course, had no idea Brenda was Tony's biological mother, as far as Charlotte knew.

The two women engaged in small talk for a while until Charlotte found a natural opening to say, "If you don't mind, I think I'll move back into the cottage here until we go down to Florida. I have a lot of work to do on the place and packing to do. It would be more convenient if I settled down here for several days. I can certainly come up to the house for meals, though."

"If you'd find that convenient, certainly," Brenda responded after a few moments of silence.

"And perhaps I'll take Sam and Rocket, if that's OK with you. You'll have your hands full with company and without any sign of housekeeping work." Charlotte almost added, "and I'll be alone," but she was afraid of what emotions that would dredge up from inside her—and perhaps in Brenda as well.

"I . . . I guess that would be sensible, yes," Brenda said, but she turned her head away from Charlotte when she said it. Charlotte couldn't have told if Brenda was disappointed or relieved—Brenda was the consummate actress—but it was done now. Charlotte didn't want to be in the middle of any family tension in Brenda's house while Tony and DeeDee were there.

"Oh, my God, Charlotte. What . . . ?"

27

Brenda had focused at last on the collapsed Wells residence. Her eyes were open wide in shock, and she was pointing to the roof smashed down on the timber of the house's flattened walls.

"Yes, the house is gone. I found it that way yesterday," Charlotte said bleakly. "That's why the dogs weren't back until today. They were fine. Sherry just had them elsewhere. The houses are down across the street too."

"Joyce Vale's rental houses?"

"Those were Joyce's houses?" Charlotte was shocked. She may be mayor of the village but she was a relative newcomer here. Although this was as much a gossip town as any sleepy village its size, newcomers weren't included in as much as the long-term residents were. Even though Brenda had moved in after she did, Brenda was returning to her childhood home, and there wasn't much about the history of the place that she hadn't heard. And Joyce Vale had lived in the village forever—or, rather, come back to her childhood home and turned it into a B&B when she and her husband retired from their high-powered New York jobs.

"Yes. And where's the construction noise coming from?"

They both looked down the river, toward the point, and, for the first time, saw that a large dock was being built out into the river from the land at the end of the point, and a dredging scow was sitting just off the point and was pulling sand up from the bottom of the river.

"That's some dock," Brenda declared. "And they're dredging the river bed up to it from the middle of the Choptank. That must be a huge yacht that they are preparing to dock there."

"Larger than a private yacht, I think."

"What in the hell is happening to our village?" Brenda said through a deep moan—a sound that disquieted both Sam and Rocket and had them nuzzling their muzzles into her lap.

"I don't know," Charlotte said grimly. "But I'm sure as hell going to find out."

* * * *

"I'm delighted you called, Charlotte. We've got a great bid on your Hopewell cottage. I hope you're sitting down."

Scooter Wilson sounded just as perky as she ever did. Scooter was Charlotte's Realtor, and she fit the stereotype right down to the ridiculous name. Charlotte had often wondered why a certain type of Realtor—the upper-middle-class, stylish, and thin-as-rail blonde who would be as delighted to decorate your new home as to sell you one for twice the price that you could afford—had perky names like Scooter or Dodo or Punky or Storm. Surely their parents hadn't seen ahead to their need for name recognition in the crowded Realtor field and helped them along. It was more likely, Charlotte thought, that these women took such "face forward" jobs to overcome the silly names they had been given.

"I feel like I've been knocked down," Charlotte answered into her phone. "Do you know what the hell is going on here in Hopewell? I haven't had time to figure it out yet. Every time I've turned around since we got home from Europe yesterday, I just see something else shocking happening."

"I've had an offer for $435,000 for the cottage. It's the riverfront property they want, of course. But this was well over—" Scooter hadn't even been listening to Charlotte's questions.

"No."

"No, what?" Scooter answered in surprise after a breath-intaking pause. Charlotte could hear the brakes of her Realtor's semitrailer mind squealing.

"No to any deal until I figure out what's going on here in Hopewell. Do you know houses are already being knocked down and land cleared? Is somebody trying to put in a Wal-Mart before we catch on to what's happening to us down here? It's not just because I'm a home owner, Scooter. I'm the mayor. I need to know what's happening."

"Umm, well. Nobody's actually officially said, mind you. It's all hush, hush. But . . ."

"But what? Spill."

"The strong rumor is that a resort is going in there, radiating out from that parcel Winston Engleton has at the end of River Street, on the point—or had. His has changed hands."

That was a rather delicate way of saying that a spy chief—the aforementioned Winston Engleton—who was supposed to be dead, missing from a fishing jaunt on the Choptank River, wasn't really dead but, rather, was part of some cat and mouse international scheme and was alive enough to have sold his property. Charlotte didn't pursue that, though. What she asked instead was, "A resort? What kind of resort?"

"I haven't heard. Something exclusive, though. I hear they're calling it The Point. Some firm from New York. When I got the offer on your cottage, I did try to trace them. But I haven't managed to do that yet." The last sentence was added as what seemed to be a somewhat reluctant afterthought, and Charlotte wasn't at all sure she believed it.

"And that's all you know?" Charlotte repeated.

"Well. I understand the Vales are involved somehow. Joyce Vale specifically. You might ask her."

"Damn right I'll ask her," Charlotte muttered.

"And now, Charlotte. About the offer. It's an excellent—"

"As I said, no. Not a never no, but a no until I am told more about what is going on here. My land is right in the middle of what they're already doing here. It's my leverage for getting some straight and complete answers. And you can pass that on to whoever is making the offer to you. It's no until and unless I get some straight and complete answers. And it better be soon, because I'm off to Florida in two weeks and I have no idea when I'll be back."

* * * *

"Joyce says she doesn't really want to talk about it."

Charlotte had ambushed Todd Vale at the side of his B&B, when she found him hammering a shutter back in place. As she had approached, two thug-looking men had brushed past her, making a belated effort to turn their faces from her when they saw her approach, and had left in a black sedan parked at the curb. She was being tugged along by Sam and Rocket on their leashes, and they both growled, evidently not liking the look of the men any better than Charlotte did. The dogs didn't normally react this way to strangers; Charlotte marked it up to good taste that they did so know, and, even though neither of the men had made a threatening move or gesture, she was glad that she had the dogs with her.

"The two houses across River Street," Charlotte honed in on Todd. "The two that have been demolished. I hear they belong to Joyce."

"They did. She's sold them, though."

"To who?"

"You'd have to ask her. I'll ask her if she's willing to tell you. But—" Todd looked very uncomfortable. He and Charlotte got along just fine. But his wife didn't feel the same way. One of Charlotte's investigations had exposed a crime that Joyce's daughter had been involved in—and Joyce's daughter had died, although entirely because of her own decisions. None of this had been Charlotte's fault, but that hadn't mattered much to Joyce.

"But you don't think she'll tell me. Something big is going on in this town, Todd—something that might destroy us as a town. I'm not just being nosy. I own a house in the way of what's coming down, and I'm mayor. And you're on the town council. I've already called a meeting of the council, and you're going to have to decide whether you are going to uphold your responsibility to the community or not."

Todd continued to look miserable. Charlotte thought he'd do his duty, though.

"Joyce hasn't told me much about the sale either, but I can tell you who handled it."

"Scooter Wilson?"

"Yes, that's right."

"And those men who I just saw leaving. Who were they?"

"Just guests. Joyce checked them in. I haven't really noticed them until now. They've stayed here before."

Yes I know they've stayed here before, Charlotte screamed internally. She didn't say it out loud, though. "Do you think they may have something to do with the land deals and demolition and construction going on around here?"

"I don't know. Maybe. Their car has New York plates. And somehow I think . . . well . . ."

"Day after tomorrow night at 8 p.m. at the community center, Todd. And you might bring Joyce if you don't want to be put on the spot yourself. I'll have Chuck Dawson there."

"The town lawyer?" Todd was dismayed.

"Yes—that's why we're not having it tomorrow; Chuck can't make a meeting until the day after—and Brenda Boynton's financial administrator will be present too. We don't know yet that whoever is bulldozing that wooded lot across the street has the right to do so. And it has Brenda terribly upset—which, Todd, means that I'm terribly upset too. Joyce has every reason to know why Brenda would be upset to see that land developed. Joyce was here when Brenda's mother was murdered there. So, Todd, day after tomorrow at 8 p.m. and come prepared to share what you and Joyce know about what's going on—or come prepared for a fight."

As Charlotte was leaving, she was thinking of those two men who had come out of the B&B and gotten into their black Lincoln sedan with the New York plates. She had recognized the car from before she'd gone to Europe, but there were enough black sedans like this that it hadn't struck a bell—not until the two men came out of the Vales's B&B. The men she recognized. They had followed her a couple

33

of weeks ago—from Hopewell, after leaving the Vales's B&B, to Ocean City—when she was tied up with investigating an Eastern Shore casino scam her former husband, Sydney, had been involved in. Those two men had been tailing her then. Her old FBI office in Annapolis had found that they were connected to New York Mafia mobsters.

New York was coming up a lot now. She'd have to call the Annapolis FBI office—something she really didn't want to do—and see if the dots were being connected again. She didn't want to do it, because an old flame of hers, Evan Worthington, was now the head of that office. And he'd been suggesting that they reconnect. Charlotte kept telling herself that she didn't want to reconnect with Evan. She was head over heels with Brenda. But her emotions weren't completely in accord with her intellectual desires. Evan was the last person she wanted to see again at least until after her trip to Florida, when that possibility had completely cooled.

She was punching numbers into her cell phone as Sam and Rocket pulled her across the street to Brenda's house. "Scooter, it's me, Charlotte Diamond, again. Before I consider selling my house, among the information I must have is who bought Joyce Vale's houses on River Street near the point. Todd Vale says you were the broker. And I also forgot to ask when I spoke to you before whether you rented out my cottage."

"Rented out your cottage? No. I would have informed you first before renting it to anyone. I know we discussed rental, but . . . why do you ask?"

"Because I've been inside, and someone is living there. The neighbor says it's a couple."

"I know nothing about that."

"Well, I will know something about it pretty soon. And about Joyce Vale's properties."

"OK, it's a matter of public record anyway. It was the Vario Construction Company."

"Of New York?"

"Yes."

"And is that who is making the offer on my cottage?"

"Good news on that front. I've been in contact with the buyer, and he says he's willing to go to $450,000 on his offer. Doesn't that sound like—?"

"No."

"No?"

"That's right. Not a yes yet. I'm still gathering information. I still want to know what's going on. You arrange a meeting between me and the buyer and maybe I'll be willing. And you didn't confirm that it's the Vario Construction Company that wants to buy my property too."

"Yes, it is." If Charlotte had ever heard a reluctant admission before, this one topped that. "We'll see what I can arrange about a meeting." Scooter continued, sounding exasperated moving toward annoyed. But she quite evidently was trying to hold herself in. The commission on selling Charlotte's property near the point in Hopewell was well worth hanging in there on politeness.

"Yes, you do that . . . please. And another question. Did you handle a sale on the Wells house—next door to mine?"

"Umm, yes." Charlotte could tell that Scooter did not want to answer these questions but that she was caught in a web of not wanting to lose Charlotte's sale. Charlotte was quite right that her house was key to expanding the land acquisition up River Street.

"And was it to the Vario Construction Company too?"

A hesitant "Yes."

"So, you've been in contact with the Wellses?" Charlotte hadn't been since the two had left Sam with her and gone to Mexico on another archeological dig. They had returned briefly from a Turkey dig before Charlotte and Brenda went to Hollywood for Brenda's last motion picture, and they'd said they were home for good. But in a matter of just days they'd left again, saying they were going to Mexico and hadn't left a contact number. They'd told Charlotte they would do so, but sometime between sunset and dawn one day, they were just gone. Charlotte had been wanting to get in contact with them, because she wanted Sam to be her dog and the question was up in the air on whether they'd come home and take him back. At this point this wouldn't just break her heart if they did. It would break Brenda's as well.

"No. Not exactly."

"Then how did you manage the sale?"

"They've had a sell order on the house for years—for a couple of years even before you moved here."

This was certainly the first time Charlotte had heard that her neighbors had wanted to leave Hopewell.

Charlotte reached the steps to Brenda's house just as Brenda opened the door. She pulled quickly back into the foyer, while Charlotte did what she could to hold the two dogs back from leaping on Charlotte. Somehow Charlotte got around her, despite Rocket uncharacteristically growling as they passed the door into the living room, and to the basement door to put the husky and boxer down in the room that had been equipped and furnished just for them.

Increasingly Brenda and Charlotte had been spending their evening in this room too, where all four were content with each other's company.

Brenda was standing at the top of the basement stairs when Charlotte came up.

"You missed a call while you were walking Sam and Rocket."

"Who from?" Charlotte asked. "Did they leave a name?"

"It was the governor's office. He said he was the governor's chief of staff."

"Oh, Lord, what could Ted Jamison want?"

"And that's not the only one looking for you. And don't be mad, but I like him."

"Like who? Ted Jamison?"

"No. Ron Rendel. He's in the living room. He said something about you holding out on him again on a news scoop."

"Double damn," Charlotte muttered. Just what they needed. The top investigative reporter with the *Baltimore Sun*. But on second thought, maybe it *was* just what she needed. Maybe the media shedding light on whatever was happening here would be just exactly what was needed. Maybe Ron could unearth whatever the thugs from New York were doing here faster than she could.

"Ron," she said with feigned surprise when she entered the living room, knowing now why Rocket had growled in passing. "I thought you'd left for the West Coast. At least that's what Sadie Hucklemeyer told me the last time I talked to her." Hucklemeyer was Rendel's editor at the *Sun*, and when Ron had gotten too close to figuring out what was up in the recent disappearance of Charlotte's neighbor on the property on the point, the retired CIA counterintelligence chief Winston Engleton, Ron had suddenly left the area.

"Reports of my permanent banishment were exaggerated," Rendel said, with a laugh. "It appears the intelligence community heat is off now, and I'm back here to see what you can do for me."

"Perhaps it's something we can do for each other," Charlotte said. "And I'm sorry about the dog growling at you. His previous owner didn't like reporters much." Rocket's previous owner had been Winston Engleton, who, indeed, had never heard a reporter's question that he had wanted to answer honestly.

"I'll get coffee," Brenda said from the hallway. It was the first time in twenty-four hours that Charlotte had heard the effervescence in Brenda's voice. She seemed to think there was something they could do about the situation now. Charlotte certainly hoped so.

Chapter Three: Bodies in the Woods

Charlotte had no idea how long the phone had been ringing before it registered with her, but it seemed insistent, so she dragged herself up from a dream that seemed ominous. But, as with most dreams, it had been so hazy and incoherent that she couldn't identify more than a few nonsensical snatches of it once she was awake. She had put earplugs in, not wanting to be awakened by the bulldozer next door, so the ringing was only on the edge of her consciousness and had somehow merged logically with her dream. She blindly reached out and connected with the telephone receiver and gave a sigh of relief when she found that lifting the receiver made the ringing stop. She almost dropped it back in the cradle but was brought into full consciousness by the "Hello? Hello? Is this Charlotte Diamond?" she heard faintly coming from down the line.

She brought the receiver to her ear, wondering who would call her in the dark of night. The receiver pushed the eye shield she'd been wearing askew, though, and she came completely up from the depths of grogginess when she realized that it wasn't dark; the morning sunshine was streaking in from windows on two walls of the bed chamber.

Next to her, Brenda muttered something in half sleep and turned over, pulling the sheet and coverlet with her.

"Yes, this is she," Charlotte answered.

"It's Ted. I hope I didn't call you too early."

Charlotte's first response was that, yes, he'd awakened her from a deep sleep; her second was to catch herself in acknowledgment that the dream she'd been having—whatever it was, something about airplanes and missing people—had been one she should be grateful to be rescued from; her third was to push the eye patch all of the way off, look at the bedside clock, and to be aghast that it was nearly 10:30 in the morning. They'd both been tired, certainly, and there was the time change from their Europe trip that had their systems flummoxed, but both she and Brenda had assumed that the bulldozing next door would have them awake and cursing by 9:00 a.m.

"Ted who?" was what she chose to say, however.

"Ted Jamison—Governor O'Malley's chief of staff. I told somebody there I'd be calling. A beautiful, haunting voice she had."

"Oh, that was Brenda. Brenda Brandon to you."

"The movie star?"

"Yes, the same."

"And you know her?"

"Yes," Charlotte answered, but what she was thinking was how shocked he might be to know just how well Charlotte knew Brenda.

"She's staying with you?"

"More like I'm staying with her. She lives in Hopewell now, you know."

"No, I didn't. That's very interesting. The governor will be surprised and pleased; he's a big fan of hers."

40

"And she's one of his constituents now," Charlotte said.

"We must have her to Annapolis for—"

"Yes, we must someday," Charlotte cut in. "But you apparently were calling to contact me." Normally Charlotte wouldn't be testy about how easily people looked right through her to see Brenda when she was in the room. But her defense was that he'd just awakened her from a deep sleep.

"Yes, indeed I did. The governor is curious whether you had considered his request to appoint you to the Gambling Commission."

"Ah, yes, I thought I'd said that I couldn't because—"

"Because your husband—your former husband—had bought a casino in Ocean City, yes. But I understand he no longer is connected with that. And the governor is very interested that you take the chair of—"

"The chair? He wants me to chair the commission?"

"Yes, that's right. With your FBI background, you have just the right credentials—and it wouldn't be a political appointment, so there should be no opposition in the legislature. The governor isn't anxious to have a fight there at the moment."

"I'm sorry, I thought that appointment no longer was in play."

"But you'll think of it now and get back to me soon?"

"Yes, yes, of course." Charlotte had been racking her brain for a reason why she couldn't do it, but she couldn't think of one now. And beyond that, she couldn't think of any reason she shouldn't do it. But she still wasn't awake enough to commit at this point. Before it hadn't just been that her former husband, Sydney, owned a Maryland casino—or, more correctly, was fronting for a crime syndicate that owned a Maryland casino—but, subsequently, because Brenda had bought a

41

piece of the casino as well. Charlotte could hardly either take the state Gambling Commission appointment if her lover was connected to gambling or to tell the governor why she couldn't. Brenda's connection had been the result of a scam and the scammer, Sydney himself and his wife, had absconded and the whole casino operation had collapsed. So, now that she thought about it, Charlotte couldn't see any reason she couldn't take the position.

She'd been trained to government work, where you serve when asked, if at all possible. So, she supposed she'd take this position—and, if not this one, something else if it came up. Her old flame, Evan Worthington, wanted her to reaffiliate with the Annapolis FBI office, and being close to him was too much of a danger, so she thought it best to accept some other offer.

"Who was that?" Brenda asked, as she turned back to Charlotte.

God, how can you look so beautiful even after a long night's sleep, Charlotte thought when she looked down into Brenda's face. "The governor's office. Don't be surprised if the next call is an invitation to you to be the centerpiece at the Governor's Ball."

"Wonderful," Brenda responded, giving a grimace that was as charming and as much a motion picture icon as her smile. "So much for living quietly in Hopewell. I . . . ." She paused there. "Why is it so quiet?" She was looking at the time on the clock. "Why isn't the bulldozer making a racket?"

"I don't know," Charlotte said, aware that Brenda was right, there was no noise coming from the neighboring lot. But before she could continue, the doorbell was ringing downstairs, Sam and Rocket were going off to bark heaven, someone was hammering on the door, and both women were dragging out of bed and pulling on their robes.

42

* * * *

"Sorry to disturb you, Ms. Diamond, Ms. Boynton. But we seem to have a problem."

Charlotte was the first to the door, and shortly thereafter Brenda, who had gone to quiet the dogs, was hovering in the background at the foot of the stairs. Facing Charlotte on the porch was the sheriff of Talbot County, Haws Wainwright. A couple of steps below him was another man, in a black trench coat, and down on the ground, looking very apprehensive and embarrassed even though he was the only one of the three Charlotte was happy to see, was David Burch, one of the county deputy sheriffs. David was the deputy charged with keeping track of this region of the county. Charlotte considered him a first-rate police officer and a good friend; the women of the county considered him the most eligible catch on the Eastern Shore.

The sheriff had his hat in his hand. He wasn't given to humility, but Charlotte had caught him in a serious transgression during a burglary and murder case a few months earlier, and Wainwright was fully aware that he could easily have lost his job if Charlotte had gone after him. Beyond that, he would walk softly around her anyway on the basis of her credentials and reputation as a senior FBI agent.

"This here is—" Wainwright started to say, gesturing toward the man on the stairs behind him.

"Tom Drexel. I know," Charlotte completed. "From the Annapolis FBI office. We haven't formally met. You came on board after I'd left. But Evan Worthington has told me about you, and I've seen you in the office."

43

"Yes, ma'am," Drexel responded in a quiet voice, full of respect. He obviously knew both of Charlotte's reputation with the FBI and the personal interest his boss took in her.

"The FBI?" Charlotte said to Wainwright, with raised eyebrow.

"Mr. Drexel was teaching a seminar at the sheriff's office this morning when we got the call. When I mentioned you and who had called, he insisted on coming with us."

"The call?"

"Yes, ma'am. It seems like déjà vu all over again. But do you remember me coming here a couple of months ago?"

"Yes, of course I . . . we do. But . . ."

"It was about a body found in Ms. Boynton's lot next door. Well, I'm afraid it's something like that again."

"A body?" Brenda exclaimed from behind Charlotte, and she drew closer to the door, her hand fluttering to her neck. The body that had been found there recently wasn't what had knocked her off her pins. Her mind was going back decades ago to when her mother's body was found in those woods.

"Well, more than one. Maybe several—actually, maybe more than several. The man from the construction company unearthed more than one body in there early this morning. He called the sheriff's office. When Tom here heard that he was employed by the Vario Construction company, he decided the Bureau might have an interest. By the time we got here, the count was up to about a dozen."

Charlotte turned and looked at Brenda. So that was why they didn't hear the bulldozer this morning, she thought. "You OK, Brenda?"

"Yes . . . I . . . I think so."

"So, I understand the lot next door has been in your family for some time?" The sheriff was looking at Brenda.

"Forever . . . or, so I thought," Brenda responded in a faraway voice.

"The ownership is in dispute, Haws," Charlotte interjected. "The construction company that's leveling it now may own it; it certainly thinks it does. And what is it about the Vario company that piqued your interest, Tom?"

"But in years past? How long have you owned it?" the sheriff asked. He was still looking directly at Brenda. Charlotte could see that he was gauging Brenda's responses.

"For generations," Brenda answered. "The land has been in my family for generations."

"The Vario construction company belongs to a major Mafia family from out of New York, Ms. Diamond," Drexel responded to the question she'd asked him. "They've been in the FBI's sights for some time. We're very interested in what they may be doing here."

"As you can see if you look up and down the street, Tom," Charlotte said, "they are into some sort of heavy development here. So far they are in the knock-down phase. We're just back from a trip to Europe, and I'm trying to find out what's going on here—I'm mayor of Hopewell. But so far I haven't pieced it all together."

"On first, brief inspection, the bodies—no more than skeletons now—appear to have been there for a long time," Sheriff Wainwright continued on the other line of discussion. "And it doesn't look like they were in coffins. We're waiting for the medical examiner—and more help. It looks like we'll need to do some extensive digging."

45

"I . . . I don't know what to say," Brenda murmured. Charlotte could see how much distress Brenda was in. She was always so poised—and never at a loss of just the right thing to say. Charlotte laid a hand on her arm, but then, seeing a car draw up to in front of the house and recognizing who was inside, she pulled her hand back and stepped away from her companion.

"The man working the bulldozer said you really seemed distressed that he was working on the lot, Ms. Boynton."

"Well, of course she was," Charlotte exclaimed with a snort. "She thought it belonged to her. And there's more about that lot, Haws—in Brenda's mind. You should know that. We've been there before."

"Yes, so it seems. But you are planning to be in residence here for the foreseeable future, aren't you?" Again, Haws was addressing Brenda directly. But it was Charlotte who answered.

"We are both off to Florida for a movie shoot in two weeks."

"We'll see about that," Wainwright said. The words were authoritative, but the tone was tentative. He knew full well what he was dealing with in both women. He wasn't at all sure that he could hold either one of them here unless he uncovered a great deal of evidence to back an accusation up.

Brenda wasn't saying anything—or listening to what Wainwright said. The focus of her attention had gone out toward the street, beyond Wainwright, Drexel, and Burch.

"Hello all. Quite a welcoming committee."

The voice was cheery and breezy—and a well-modulated baritone. It was as if sunshine had pushed away the clouds and the world had returned from the brink of gloom and doom.

Tony Trice, with DeeDee Yance, had arrived at Brenda's village mansion.

Brenda seemed to be shrinking into the shadows. She was clutching her robe tightly to her and giving a wild look at Charlotte.

Charlotte moved to between her and the door. "Hello, Tony. Welcome DeeDee. These gentlemen were just leaving. And I must go too. I had just arrived before they showed up. I woke up this morning to find I was out of coffee. Major catastrophe. I can't function until I've had my coffee. These gentlemen were just leaving, and I'll be off as soon as my need for caffeine beans has been satisfied. Bring your bags right in. I'm sure Brenda has rooms set up for you upstairs. Welcome to Hopewell."

After the unnecessary trip to the kitchen for a bag of coffee, Charlotte was backing out of the front door. She doubled around to the back of the house where there was a door into the ground-level basement. There was a dog run beside the door stoop with a dog door into Sam and Rocket's special room, but both dogs were outside and panting at the fence, ready to go anywhere Charlotte was willing to take them.

"Guess it's just you guys and me for a while," Charlotte said, as she leashed them up. If either dog felt the sadness in her voice, they weren't letting on. "None of us will have it as well at my cottage as we do here, I'm afraid," she added.

She still got no reaction. There are times, she thought, that she'd like to have life as simple and uncomplicated as Sam and Rocket had it.

* * * *

As she walked up River Street in her robe and slippers, holding a full can of gourmet coffee beans in her hand and being pulled along by Sam and Rocket, Charlotte's mind was racing on what, if any, wardrobe she had at Diamond Cottage—and whether there was anything there appropriate to this season. And cosmetics and toothpaste. Could she somehow slip her things out of Brenda's house without Tony and DeeDee seeing them, or did she need to make a trip to the drug store? She hoped her small hybrid SUV, the Escape, would start. It had been locked in her garage while they were in Europe, and she hadn't had time to check on it. But it was fairly new. It should be fine.

She was almost at her cottage before she saw that there was a car parked in the driveway. And she only looked up then because Rocket was letting out a bark. He somehow had known that she needed to be warned about something.

Oh, god, not that too, she thought. This wasn't the time or the circumstance to be confronting whoever had been using her house. But if that was their car, at least she wouldn't have to track them down. With everything else that was going wrong, she might as well be having this confrontation. She was in the mood to do battle.

"Sydney!"

She saw him as soon as she opened the door, and she had to hold off Rocket from lunging at him. Sam seemed more curious about the tantalizing mixtures of orders in the air, most of which Charlotte would like to pretend weren't there.

Sydney was sitting at the dining room table, drinking a cup of the coffee she had just said she didn't have in the house. Charlotte's mind raced back two years. It was like there had been no brief separation, no quick divorce. He looked as much the morning slouch as ever, sitting there in his pajama bottoms and tattered robe.

"Oh, god," he said, coffee splashing out of his mug as it hit the surface of the table. "I thought you were in Europe. And when did you get those monster mutts?"

"I wasn't going there to live, Sydney. It was just for Christmas. It's January now. What in the hell are you doing in my house? Or even the country."

"We weren't going to be here long. We just were checking something for Delores's uncle and then we'll be out of the country."

"I thought Delores's uncle was after your scalp—literally—for the scam you were running on that casino he thought he owned."

"Oh, that's all smoothed over. Delores fixed that. Blood is thicker and all that, you know."

"I know the police are after you too—and I should shoot you on site for the kidnapping stunt you pulled on Brenda. So, what are you doing for your new wife's uncle, Sydney? You can come on out, Delores. I see you there in the hallway. I won't bite—although Sam and Rocket might. Here, while you two get your lies straight, I'll put the dogs in the back bedroom. Neither one of them seems to like you much. And for this I could give each a hug."

Delores, Sydney's secretary when Sydney was married to Charlotte and now his wife, slithered into the room and took a seat at the table beyond Sydney, where they were both sitting, Sydney looking at the wall and Delores at her manicure, when Charlotte returned. Charlotte wanted to strangle Delores for the scam and snatch she and Sydney had perpetrated on Brenda and her in the Ocean Front Hotel and Casino scheme, but she never could get too mad at Delores.

49

Delores was married to Sydney now. That seemed to Charlotte to be punishment enough to cover a whole range of crimes.

Sydney just sat there, looking alternately scared and contemplative of what he could tell Charlotte. She knew he certainly wouldn't tell her the truth, if he could help it. Never the truth if it could be avoided. There was no fun or challenge for him in that.

"I asked what you two are doing for Uncle Joe Crea here that entices you to be where warrants are out on you."

"It's not Crea himself," Sydney said. "We're here for an associate of his."

"Paul Vario?" Charlotte asked. She was taking a shot in the dark, but the surprised look on Sydney's face told her she'd hit the mark. She pressed in, using the advantage that he didn't know how much else she knew. "Are you checking on the construction going on here for Vario?"

"How did you know that?" Delores piped up and asked. Sydney gave his wife a dirty look and emitted a low hiss. Delores shrank back in her chair.

"Never mind how I knew that. What's going on here, Sydney?"
Sydney was buttoning his lips.

"Delores. What's going on here?" Charlotte walked over to the kitchen phone and took the receiver off the hook. "One call and you both will be in prison tonight."

"No. Don't, please," Delores said, with a catch in her throat. "It's a resort. The Vario family is putting an exclusive resort in here."

"Family fun? The Vario family? You can do better than that, Delores."

50

They all heard the sound of an automobile pulling up outside, and Charlotte walked over to the window. What she saw made her do a double take.

"It's the chief of the Annapolis FBI bureau, Evan Worthington," Charlotte said.

"You're joking," Sydney snorted. Then he laughed, a nervous laugh that gave him away.

"Have you ever known me to joke about something like that, Sydney?"

Now he looked scared.

"Please, Charlotte," Delores pleaded. "Not here, not now. It's a casino the Varios are putting in. Not a public one, of course, but a big one—for high rollers. It's to be called The Point. They'll bring the clients in by boat—all hush, hush. They want as much of the land around here as they can get."

"OK, you two in the back for now. I'll see what he wants. But you have to turn yourselves in, you know."

As the two scurried back to the bedrooms, Charlotte straightened her robe and went to the door.

"Hi, Charlotte."

"You didn't need to come, Evan. I'm sure the bodies found in that lot have nothing to do with me. I'm betting it was a native American burial ground—that it will turn out just to be that."

"That's not what brought me down here, Charlotte. There was another call. Too many coincidences."

"What?"

"I'll explain on the way. I need you to come with me, if you will."

51

"Like this?"

"I'll take you any way I can get you," he said, with a sardonic smile. But then he added, "If you want to get dressed, please be quick about it. They need us down at the river."

Oh, lord, what can this be about? Charlotte thought, as she went back to the bedrooms, silently moved Sydney and Delores from the master bedroom to her office den, and then frantically went through her drawers and the closet—pushing Sydney's and Delores's clothes aside—looking for something appropriate to wear.

Both Charlotte and Evan got into the backseat of a black Escalade SUV he'd been driven up in. A young agent Charlotte had never met was driving, and Evan didn't introduce her. Contrary to his promise, Evan also didn't tell Charlotte what was up, and she didn't ask, being nervous at being in the backseat of an automobile with the hunky FBI agent. The last time they had been in this position, the windows had been steamed up. Luckily, they only had to drive as far as into Winston Engleton's former walled acreage at the end of River Street on the point.

The SUV drove up to the new dock the Vario construction company was building, where it stopped and Evan and Charlotte got out.

Charlotte looked out onto the water and her heart came up into her throat. Suspended between the dock and the dredging scow was a dripping-wet sedan held in the air by the crane from the scow.

"They found this while they were dredging, Charlotte. You're a resident here. I thought you might recognize the car."

"I do."

"There are two bodies inside. A man and a woman. The medical examiner is up at the lot next to Brenda Boynton's but will be

52

down here soon to take a look at them. I don't think they've been in there more than a month, though. Whose car is it?"

"It belongs to my neighbors, Anne and Bill Wells. They are supposed to be in Mexico on an archeological dig. I saw them about three weeks ago. They had just returned from Turkey—and then took off for Mexico in the middle of the night."

"They may not have gone as far as Mexico."

Chapter Four: Lose Neighbors and Gain a Housekeeper

While Charlotte and Evan were standing by the water as the crane from the scow swung the Wellses' Toyota sedan over onto the dock, another black SUV drove up and Sharon Como, the county medical examiner climbed out. Charlotte liked and respected the woman and, unlike many in the county, gave her latitude for being abrupt and somewhat morose because of the grim jobs she was called in to perform.

"So, what do we have up at the top of the street, Sharon?" Evan asked. Sharon had worked down in Virginia when Charlotte and Evan were at Quantico, where the FBI training and research facilities were located, so the three had known each other for quite some time.

"I don't know yet. They are still unearthing bodies, I'm sorry to say. Some in single graves, some in twos and threes. The bodies aren't recent, but they don't appear to be ancient, either."

"No chance it's something as natural as a Native American burial site?" Charlotte asked, hoping that this might be the case.

"There's always that possibility, I suppose," Sharon answered. Her voice made her sound either tired or slightly piqued. Charlotte went with tired whereas many in the county would say that the woman was just on edge and touchy—and would back off from talking with her and probably miss out on some very astute observations. "But I've studied some of the Native American customs of the tribes that were in this area, and this just doesn't seem to be a familiar burial pattern. Typically I would have expected mounds and shell circles marking the area. The trees look like an old stand. You live here, Charlotte. Do you have any idea whether the lot has any cultural history?"

"No. I haven't lived here very long. Brenda Boynton, who lives in the old federal mansion next to the lot, says it's been in her family for generations, and her family has been here from the beginning of European settlement of Maryland. It's never been developed as far as she knows. It's a little peculiar, though, because the rest of this side of the Choptank has been developed up to the river. Maybe she knows if there's a connection with Native Americans."

"Anyone in town who might know more of the history than this Boynton woman? Has she been here since birth? How old is she?"

"Brenda has returned here more recently than I've moved here," Charlotte answered. "She's the movie star, Brenda Brandon, and has been off in Hollywood much of her life. Her house was shut up for decades, with her paying to have it maintained. Her father moved to New York soon after Brenda went to Hollywood."

"Ah, so she hasn't been much in touch," Sharon said.

"There are some residents of the village who have been here longer," Charlotte said, starting to tax her brain for who might be useful. "Joyce Vale, who owns the B&B across the street from the lot is a childhood resident. But she was off in New York, working at a publishing house, for most of her life too. There are some older long-term residents." Then her mind chinked into place. "There's Hannah Helgerson over on Spring Street, the extension beyond Main Street. She's as old as the hills, and, as I remember, she said her grandfather was a blacksmith here and her father a farrier after that. I don't think she ever moved away for any length of time. I'll go over there as soon as we're done here. Hannah's always spouting off village folklore at community meetings. If anyone knows a history for the lot, it will be Hannah."

"It's a pity that Brenda Brandon doesn't know more about it," Evan interjected.

Charlotte snorted. "Brenda didn't even know that she didn't own the lot—that it hadn't come to her from her father with all of the other property he held. And she knows more about the lot than she really wants to," Charlotte added.

"How so?" Sharon's voice showed her interest.

"Brenda's mother was murdered on the river bank on that lot—and Brenda found the body. You can imagine how traumatic that would be for a young girl. That, plus a more recent murder there has all of the residents avoiding the place."

"Ah, so it's cursed." Sharon was smiling for the first time since she arrived. "Maybe it *is* a Native American sacred ground."

She quickly lost her smile and put on her professional face, though, because the three of them were being motioned over to the dripping Toyota that had been settled on the dock and now had its front doors pried open.

Evan and Sharon walked to the car; Charlotte was hanging back. She wasn't squeamish, but this wasn't her case—and quite likely those were her neighbors in the car. She could make out two masses in the front seat, but she would have been hard pressed to identify them as human remains without the circumstantial evidence to guide her.

Sharon started on the driver's side, while Evan worked the glove compartment on the passenger side. Then he stepped out and came back to where Charlotte stood while Sharon moved around to the passenger door.

"It's registered to a Bill Wells," he said as he drew beside Charlotte.

"Yes, that's my neighbor. And his wife's name is Anne. I'm sure that's their Toyota."

"Sharon says there's not much she can say yet other than it's a man and a woman, maybe early sixties both and maybe three or four weeks of decomp. She'll have the bodies taken back to the morgue where she'll do what she can with them. You don't know who their dentist is, do you?"

"Sorry, I can't help you there. They've been abroad virtually the whole time I've been living here. The ages match up, though—as well as the last time I saw them. As I said, they left unexpectedly in the middle of the night. I'd been watching their Siberian husky, Sam, for them, and they didn't even turn him back over to me. I woke up to him scratching at my back screen door and their car gone."

"Well, with all that's going on here—and with the Varios involved, though I don't know how exactly—we'll keep this on the FBI plate until we learn there's no federal connection. That will make access to records faster and fuller."

"I can shed light on the Vario connection," Charlotte said. "I've just learned that they are putting in a resort with a high-flyer clandestine gambling operation here on the point. They're even naming it The Point. That's why they're buying up and clearing land. They want to make the grounds as extensive and private as possible. The dock is for large boats to bring clients in from up and down the coast."

"Then an FBI operation it will be," Evan said. "We have the Varios square in our sights. If this is to be gambling, they may be giving us just the hook that we need. And if these deaths and maybe the bodies in the lot can be tagged to them . . ."

He didn't go on. He didn't need to. Charlotte had conducted high-level investigations like this herself. She was grateful, though, that he hadn't asked how she knew what the Varios were up to.

She begged off then with the excuse that she was going to pump the brain of Hannah Helgerson. But what she really wanted to do was to get back to her cottage and pin Sydney and Delores down now that she was thinking of them again.

But when she got to Diamond Cottage, she wasn't really all that surprised to find that Sydney and Delores had packed up and taken off.

As soon as she let the dogs out, they were all over the cottage. But they came when Charlotte called.

"No, I didn't like them very much either," she said to the dogs when they came to her. And even though you are just dogs, she thought, I won't tell you I was married to one of them. I don't want to come down in your estimation.

Then, looking at them looking up with her with such trust and devotion, she knelt on the floor and embraced them together. "I'm glad I at least have you two while I'm in exile from Brenda's. I have a house call to make, and if you go with me, I'm afraid you'll have to wait out on the porch. I know it's cold. So, what do you want to do?"

She had stood and reached for Sam's and Rocket's leashes, so there was no question what the dogs wanted to do. They both bounded for the front door, tails wagging and tongues lolling out of their mouths.

* * * *

"This is delicious. What *is* this lovely soup?"

"Bea says it's a chestnut soup. It is tasty, isn't it? And you should taste her butternut squash soup. That's out of this world. I declare I've put on ten pounds in the two weeks she's been here. I really need to exercise more. Of course any exercise I'd do would be more. With this bum leg of mine, exercise isn't . . ."

Charlotte was tuning Hannah Helgerson down to a dull drone at this point in an attempt to bring her back to the point Charlotte was interested in. Although, truth be known, she also was very interested in this soup Hannah's niece, Bea, had served.

Charlotte had arrived at Hannah's wooden Craftsman-style bungalow on Spring Street just in time for lunch. She hadn't planned it that way, but she only then realized how hungry she was. With the excitement at Brenda's house followed by finding her ex-husband and his new wife hiding out in her cottage and then having been taken to the dock on the point, she hadn't even had breakfast yet. She had hoped to only be at Hannah's long enough to ask her a couple of questions.

Spending time with Hannah was an invitation to an earache from overuse. But she'd arrived as Hannah was sitting down to her lunch, and she hadn't been quick enough to decline an offer to join her.

After having been served this chestnut soup, Charlotte was glad she hadn't turned down the invitation.

"About the lot next to Brenda's."

"Rumor is it's a virtual graveyard. That they are digging up bodies piled on top of bodies."

"I'm not sure it's that bad," Charlotte responded. "But that's the general gist, yes. You're probably the one in Hopewell with the longest continuous residency here—"

"Honey, I'm the oldest one in Hopewell by far," Hannah crowed. "And I ain't stepped foot out of here since 1948. Or was it '50? It was the summer Jed Clagett got run over by his plow—or, to be honest, run himself over—and my father drove him over to Easton with me in the backseat with Jed and trying to hold that leg steady in the makeshift—"

"Yes, well, since you're the oldest one here, the authorities . . ." Charlotte didn't want to send Hannah's heart racing by mentioning the presence of the FBI, ". . . wondered if you knew anything about the history of that lot. Anything that could help them. I know people shy away from it. There's the suggestion it might have been a Native American burial ground or otherwise sacred to the early tribes here."

Bea Helgerson had come into the dining room and was clearing the soup dishes away. She'd brought in a platter of tuna fish salad with her that made Charlotte's mouth water on presentation alone. She was a pleasant-looking woman who seemed to be Charlotte's age or a bit older, dressed neat as a pin, but with a sense of melancholy about her. When she reached the doorway to the kitchen, she turned and gave Charlotte a rolled-up-eyes expression that conveyed that she was just about ready to climb the walls from living with Hannah for two weeks.

60

That was the moment she could have kissed Bea, who obviously realized as Charlotte did, this wouldn't be a quick visit through no fault of Charlotte's.

"Excuse me, are those your dogs out on the porch?" she'd asked when she'd brought drinks in.

"Yes. The Siberian husky is Sam and the boxer is Rocket. I hope you don't—"

"They might catch their death of cold before we let you go," the woman said with a glance at Hannah that gave Charlotte to understand that Bea knew Hannah was likely to talk Charlotte's ear off. "If you don't mind, I'll let them in the kitchen with me. I love dogs. I bet I can even find them each a little treat."

Charlotte signaled her gratitude, while Hannah just continued rattling on.

"Indian burial ground?" Hannah laughed. "No, I never heard that. Never heard talk of no Indians in these woods. First thing I remember about those woods being some place to stay away from . . . you know that sweet Brenda's momma was murdered there and left to die right in the marshy reeds by the river, don't you? Now if that didn't raise a ruckus around here. And some folks thinking Brenda had something to do with it. But I never. That Brenda were always a sweet, beautiful child. Now her mother. She had a mouth on her and was a real pistol. And she could be a nosy little thing. And her dad with his 'first family' highfalutin' ways—"

"Your first negative memory of that wooded lot . . . ?" Charlotte interjected quietly—but without effect.

"And then just earlier this year—you were all tied up with that, so I'se sure you remember. That insurance company lady murdered, and Doctor Rachel being undone."

"The authorities are really interested in back further than any of that, Hannah. I know they'd be very grateful to you if you had information that could help them. You were saying that the woods were known as some place to stay away from when you were a child."

"Yes, they most certainly were. It all set in with Prohibition, it did. During the late twenties at first, I heard, and then I saw it with my own eyes in the late forties and into the fifties."

"Saw what with your own eyes, Hannah?"

"Cars. Always black cars. Big ones. Buicks and Cadillacs and such. Also late at night. And lights being seen in those woods. Folks would pull away from there. Kids like me would go to the corner of Penn and River and peek out from behind what became Doctor Rachel's house. And we'd see them."

"Them?"

"Those black cars and lights in the wood. We'd see them. Stopped seeing them in, let's see. Maybe the early seventies. About the time my Maybelle went off to college, I guess. I caught her out there lookin' at the cars at night when she was younger, and I tanned her hide good for it, I did. I told her, 'Maybelle, there can be no good come from being near those woods at night. Never know what sort of bad trouble you could be getting yourself into, girl.' Of course I never did tell her I'd done the same when I was her age and younger even."

Hannah stopped to giggle and to spoon a generous portion of tuna fish salad onto Charlotte's plate. And Charlotte paused to inhale the food that was as delicious to the taste as it had been to the eye when Bea had brought it in.

Hannah nudged Charlotte's arm and asked, "Ever eaten anything as divine as that salad?"

"No, I certainly haven't," Charlotte responded. Although she thought that this might not be true upon contemplation. The chestnut soup would give the salad a run for its money.

Hannah's voice lowered to a hoarse whisper. "Real tragedy it was."

"A tragedy?" Charlotte asked—thinking that Hannah had more to reveal about the wooded lot next door to Brenda's house.

"Yes. Nobody in the family would talk about it, of course, but I reckon it was a real love match. And I never begrudged Bea her happiness. Let what will be be, I said. What will be for Bea. Now that's downright funny, ain't it? 'Be' and 'Bea' right together like that." Hannah stopped to chortle at her own joke before she went on.

"Well, some of the family wouldn't have her in their house, but I always said that woman of hers seemed right nice and I didn't see no men buzzing around Bea. Buzzing bees. Ha! That's funny too. I'm on a roll today. They wasn't hurting anyone. And now the woman's dead and Bea didn't have anywhere to go. So, of course, I invited her to come stay with me until she got back on her pins. She said she wants to find a position somewhere. As a housekeeper or something. And the way she cooks. I can't imagine someone not snarfing her right up. Can you?"

"No, Hannah, I certainly can't," Charlotte responded. And nothing she'd said that day had been as heartfelt as what she'd just answered.

Bea only nailed the led down on what Charlotte was thinking when Charlotte was ready to go and found Sam and Rocket laying on the floor under the kitchen table, their tails wagging, showing their best manners, and looking up at Bea puttering calming about and talking to them like they were people. The eyes of both dogs followed Bea's movements and monologue with such interest and devotion that Charlotte knew that they appreciated the woman and her cooking as much as Charlotte had.

* * * *

On her way back to her cottage, the thought of the food she'd just had and the way the dogs were regarded and treated sent Charlotte's mind racing on what might be. It was Brenda's decision, of course, but Bea Helgerson might be the answer to what was needed at Brenda's house. Brenda would want to know what was what with Edith Smith first, Charlotte knew, so she saw her next move as pulling the Escape out of the garage and going out to Clagett's farm. It wasn't that far out of town, but it was farther than Charlotte wanted to walk and return.

After the dogs had pulled her along the short two-block stretch of stores and offices that constituted Main Street and she had reached River Street and looked beyond her cottage to the collapsed Wells house and the line of bulldozers parked at the curb, though, she was suddenly back into the world of change in her village and her thoughts returned to the mysteries of whatever the Vario family was up to and to what her neighbors—if it was Anne and Bill Wells in that car sitting on the dock at the point—had to do with any of that. She was practically at her door when it hit her. She was thinking about selling her cottage to become part of a gambling casino resort. She couldn't accept an appointment to the governor's Gambling Commission, and especially as its chair, if she had been involved in a lucrative land deal with a casino.

But it probably wouldn't come to that. The Varios apparently hadn't bothered to seek permission to set up a casino here. If what Delores had told her was true, they were doing everything they could to keep the true nature of their resort plans a secret—perhaps so interested in that that they were going to any extreme necessary to keep it secret. Perhaps that was what had happened to the Wellses. Maybe they had found out who they were selling their house to and why and threatened to expose the Varios and were silenced.

The telephone answering machine was blinking at Charlotte when she opened the door to Diamond Cottage. Her heart leaped when she heard the voice of Brenda.

"This is a plea for help. You must come to dinner. Cocktails before, of course. Save me."

She wanted both to laugh and to cry. She'd managed to forget, if only for an hour or so, about Brenda being left with the unexpected early arrival of her secret son and the ingénue he was trying to impress—but who Brenda—and Charlotte herself—found to be spoiled and a bit snotty. Charlotte wondered if her ploy to explain what she was doing at Brenda's in her pajamas and robe had convinced anyone—most specifically DeeDee Yance. Even if it had, though, Charlotte could imagine that the day had been tense at Brenda's. Tony had come because the producer of their coming movie suggested that he and Brenda go over their respective parts in the script before they arrived in Florida. DeeDee was only a "maybe" in being cast, though, so she could be counted on to be both bored—she was easily bored when she wasn't

65

in the spotlight—and pouty that she had no function other than being a "maybe" for Tony Trice, something her mother was pushing for publicity purposes, Charlotte thought, more enthusiastically than DeeDee herself seemed to be. There was no doubt that she liked Tony, but there was less doubt that she liked DeeDee the most.

Charlotte checked her watch. She had time to drive out to the Clagett farm to see what was what with Edith Smith before the cocktail hour. She'd stop at Brenda's on the way back. She briefly considered taking Sam and Rocket, but if Edith saw them coming, Charlotte would probably have to chase her into the woods to be able to say anything to her at all. So, it would be back in the bedroom for these guys. Charlotte knew they'd be OK; they'd been walked and had experienced quite a lot of adventure today already.

Charlotte was very uneasy about this Edith Smith business. She had seen her earlier the previous day scuttling around near the B&B, across the street from the wooded lot and Brenda's—or at least Charlotte hoped that was Edith. Before they'd gone on their Rhine River Christmas cruise, Charlotte had seen Edith for the first time and had mistaken her for someone else who turned out to be her look-alike cousin, Ida. Ida Smith had been the target of one of Charlotte's last FBI investigations—the only one Charlotte hadn't been able to close before she retired. She had been implicated in a series of robberies that extended across state lines, which is what had brought the FBI into the investigation, and that had concluded with the murder of an old woman who had surprised the robbers by being home when she shouldn't have been. Ida had eluded capture and had become the subject of a manhunt. When Charlotte retired to Hopewell, she was surprised to find a woman, Edith Smith, living there who looked remarkably like the elusive Ida and

66

then, when robberies occurred in Hopewell. Brenda, who had been employing Edith Smith as a part-time domestic, had been robbed.

When the results of the fingerprinting from that robbery came back, Ida was revealed to have been posing as her cousin. At the time Charlotte had been afraid that Ida had done away with Edith and taken her place, and an augmented arrest warrant had been issued for Ida. Then Charlotte and Brenda had gone out to Hollywood for one of Brenda's movie shoots and had been so embroiled in a mystery out there that Charlotte forgot all about the Smiths. When they returned, and just before they left for their Rhine River cruise, Edith Smith was back—and wanting her job back. Ida hadn't been captured and arrested, and Edith claimed that she had left a message for Brenda that she had to go take care of her ailing mother on short notice. Ida apparently had intercepted the message and taken Edith's place—and then robbed Brenda's house.

Events had thrown all of this on the backburner in Charlotte's and Brenda's minds, but now it was back front and center. Edith was supposed to have been cleaning regularly at the mansion while she and Brenda were on their Rhine cruise, but this apparently hadn't been done. There needed to be a change, but Charlotte's investigative instincts were worrying at her—wondering if perhaps Ida had shown up again and this time made Edith's disappearance more permanent.

Nothing Charlotte found at Clagett's farm reassured her or tampered down the worries at the back of her brain. No one answered the door, which wasn't locked. Charlotte went inside and saw no evidence that Edith had been there in recent days. Instead, the place looked like it had been ransacked. Before she left, she made a call to the deputy sheriff, David Burch.

"Hello, Charlotte," he answered. "Sorry about this morning. There wasn't anything I could do. I hope Ms. Brenda isn't too upset."

"I haven't seen her since then, David. But she has her movie friends with her now, so I think that will distract her from what's happening on the lot next door. And I certainly understand that the authorities had to check with us this morning. I'm afraid I'm calling for some other reason."

"Oh? What can I do for you—anything, you know."

"I'm at Clagett's farm. Looking for Edith Smith. I think you might need to get a team out here. She looks like she's gone, but, if she did, she didn't seem to take much with her. And the house has been tossed."

"You think her cousin has made another appearance?"

"It's what I'm afraid of, yes. And maybe your people should do a good search of the grounds too. I don't have a very good feeling about this."

"Your intuition is good enough for me. Can we reach you at Ms. Brenda's?"

"You should maybe try my cottage first. With Brenda's movie friends at the mansion, room is tight there. I've moved back in to the cottage temporarily."

"Got cha. I'm sorry so much is going on in the village, Ms. Charlotte."

"So am I, David. So am I."

* * * *

"Thank god you're here," Brenda whispered in a husky voice when she answered the door. Charlotte had almost just walked in and had remembered only at the last moment that she should ring the doorbell—that she was just another visitor in this fantasy script that Brenda was trying to write to provide what she believed was a more acceptable perception of her by the son she couldn't acknowledge to the world.

"How are the dogs?" Brenda asked. "I miss them."

"Good, I don't want you to stop missing them. We're a family; we belong together." Charlotte had promised herself she wouldn't say anything about having to leave the house. "And unless Tony and DeeDee see the basement room or the dog run, it's probably best not even to tell them you have dogs."

"Oh, Lord no, DeeDee won't look beyond her nose, and Tony is being attentive to DeeDee. It's been simply arctic around here," Brenda continued. "They are in the living room. We're on our second drink already, so you'll have to catch up."

"Arctic?" Charlotte asked?

"Shh. They'll hear you. Yes, decidedly icy. She thinks I'm vamping for Tony—trying to take him away from her. Honest, I'm doing nothing."

"You know how you can put an end to that, don't you? I'll bet Tony wouldn't care less. And I certainly wouldn't—for my part."

"You're no help," Brenda responded, with a grimace. "Get in there and be her mother for her. I'm afraid that might be the basic problem. It's the first time, I think, that DeeDee's mother hasn't been plastered to her hip to tell her what to do at every turn. She seems lost and is overcompensating."

"You must be desperate to call on me to sweet talk anyone," Charlotte countered.

"Just bring her into the arena," a man's smooth baritone rang out from the living room. "You're letting all of the heat out of the house."

"We're coming," Brenda sang back, using all of her acting talent to change her tone from plaintive to confident. "Or Charlotte will be in. I have to go finish burning dinner."

Charlotte then moved into the living room as Brenda split off toward the kitchen. From what Charlotte could smell in the air, Brenda wasn't lying about the burning part. But Charlotte hadn't taken up with Brenda for her cooking—and there would be no comparisons. Charlotte also was ready to concede that Brenda was a better cook than she was.

Charlotte didn't have to endure the freeze for long. She'd found DeeDee pouty and simpering and plastered up to Tony's side on a sofa in the living room, but the young woman's cell phone went off almost as soon as Charlotte had poured herself a gin and tonic, scouted out the sturdiest chair she could see in Brenda's collection of true antique furniture, and sat down.

It was DeeDee's mother—doing her every-fifteen-minute checkup from Palm Springs, and DeeDee bounced out of the room to take the call.

"Brenda has packed you up," Tony said when they were alone. "I think you'll find suitcases at the back door downstairs. She obviously doesn't want DeeDee and me to know she's done this. This is all unnecessary, you know."

"I know. But it's important to Brenda. I don't think she'd care if the world knew. At least the other world. You are her world too, though. And I think your impressions are important to her."

"Perhaps I should just come right out and tell her that I know and don't care a jot," Tony said.

"Maybe, when the moment's right," Charlotte answered. "But I don't think Brenda thinks this is the moment—not with DeeDee here."

"Well, if you can endure it, I can wait," Tony said. "But it doesn't matter a bit to me, you know. I want you to know that. I'm just pleased that she's found happiness."

"Has she, do you think?" Charlotte asked.

"Yes. I have no doubts about that—I've known her a lot longer than you have, you know. Even if I didn't know how much a part of her I am. But I can tell that there's a happiness and a sense of fulfillment in her now—since you came into the picture—that there never was before. No matter how many acting accolades she received, she always wondered how talented she really was. And there were those years when she was waiting for David Runion to notice her, and he's was only noticing the likes of me. No, you're the best thing that's ever happened to her."

"Thank you for that," Charlotte answered in a small voice. She was about to say something else but DeeDee was bouncing back and Brenda was at the door to the living room as well, announcing that the ruins of dinner could now be found on the dining room table.

Later in the evening, Brenda and Charlotte were temporarily alone because DeeDee had insisted Toy take her out to find some night life and Brenda and Charlotte were so anxious to get the tension out of the air that they didn't disabuse her of the notion that any nightlife she'd recognize as acceptable couldn't be found this side of the Atlantic shoreline, much too far away to drive to for an evening. The two woman were cuddled on the living room sofa and enjoying a quiet brandy and coffee.

"Dinner was a disaster," Brenda murmured with a sigh.

"The conversation could have gone a lot better, I agree," Charlotte responded. "If you'd like me to take DeeDee out for a sail in your Laser and be the only one to come back, I'm game."

"Don't tempt me. But Tony likes her."

"No, I'm not so sure. Tony isn't as dumb as you might think."

"I meant the meal, of course. I can't cook worth spit."

"I didn't suffer," Charlotte said. She paused but then surged ahead. "A failed dinner is fine because I had a divine lunch."

"You did? Surely not something you fixed at the cottage."

"No, of course not. You know my cooking skills better than that. No, I was at Hannah Helgerson's for lunch. She has a niece living with her at least temporarily who is a fantastic cook."

"Lucky Hannah."

"I think it could be lucky us. I said temporarily. I think Bea— that's her name, Bea Helgerson—would make a great housekeeper for us. You should have seen her with Sam and Rocket. I think they worship her on the basis of only one meeting—and see genuinely seems to like dogs."

"But there's Edith Smith."

"Who isn't anything at all like the housekeeper we need—and who is scared silly of Sam and Rocket. I went out to see Edith, and she isn't at the farm—and I don't really expect that she'll be back. No, I think Bea Helgerson might be the ticket for us."

"Isn't she here to take care of Hannah? What sort of incentive could we offer?"

"You mean other than taking care of two glamorous old dames?" Charlotte laughed, and so did Brenda then. Charlotte was happy to hear the signature tinkling laughter from Brenda. She hadn't heard it all evening. "No, she is here because she lost her significant other—and you have that separate suite downstairs that would be just perfect for a live-in housekeeper. And I have a feeling that separate living quarters from Hannah is all the incentive Bea would need."

"But the arrangements here. Having—"

"Her significant other was a woman."

"Ah." The two women were both silent for several minutes before Brenda spoke again. "About the arrangements . . . tossing you out like that this morning, Charlotte. I'm sorry. I just couldn't—"

"Whatever makes you comfortable. But Tony might be more open to our relationship than you think, Brenda. And I highly suspect that Tony is the only one who concerns you in this regard."

"I know it's terribly unfair of me. And nonsensical too. I'm sure that in time I . . ."

"It's OK, Brenda. It's no big deal. Sure, in time. Whenever you are ready."

Charlotte tried to sound nonchalant, but she was sure she hadn't been convincing. She couldn't deny her disappointment—at least to herself. She'd continue to tell Brenda that it didn't hurt that Brenda wasn't able yet to declare their relationship to the world. But it wouldn't really be an honest relationship until they were able to do that.

Who was she to put it all on Brenda, though? Wasn't she anxious for it all to come out in the open primarily because she was afraid of her feelings for Evan Worthington—how he made her heart rush every time they met and how he was pursuing her again after all of these years? Didn't she want the door closed on any heterosexual relationships out of fear that until it was she would always be susceptible to the charms of Evan or some another man?

She turned to Brenda and smiled. "I tell you what. I'm so committed to you that I'm going to volunteer to chip the charcoal off the sides of that casserole dish you served for dinner. What was that you were serving, by the way?"

"Bitch!" Brenda exclaimed, and she turned and swatted Charlotte on the arm. And then there was that lilting laughter again. The Brenda Charlotte loved was back.

"So, can I call Bea Helgerson tomorrow and pitch her on a full-time, live-in job?"

"If you think it's too late to do so tonight."

"No, I don't think it's ever too late to throw out a life preserver."

Chapter Five: History Returns to Haunt

A motley crew, otherwise known as the Hopewell on the Choptank town council, gathered in a cold—both in temperature and atmosphere—room in the community center on River Street. It was a room where white-painted cinderblock walls and institutional green linoleum-tiled floors were garishly offset by an exhibit of angry-colored abstract paintings rendered by the town clerk, Mary Miller, to whom no one had had the nerve to give an honest artistic critique. As with any small village, the community center's rooms were multipurpose. This one served both as city council chamber and community art gallery and the workshop of the ladies flower-arranging monthly workshop—and, when someone got the crazy notion to put on a pageant or concert, it served as an auditorium as well.

Although Charlotte, as mayor, had called an irregular meeting of the council, all of the usual attendees were there, whether or not they were either on the council or had been invited to the meeting. Mary Miller, as town clerk, had to be there to take notes. And Charlotte had to remind her that this is what she was there for, as Mary seemed more interested in explaining her artistic inspiration and motivation for this painting or that on the wall to various town councilors—when, left to their own devices—they most like would have speculated that Mary's paintings came out of a bad hair day in which she'd slammed her hand in a car door.

Straggling in too, were Jason Williams, operator of the Hopewell automobile garage; Hannah Helgerson, not elected but never turned away on the strength of being the authority on what had happened when in the village; and the Episcopal pastor, Don Dunkel, a fixture at anything connected with the village. Nearly the last to roll in was Bonny Levitt, trying to outlive Hannah Helgerson as senior Hopewell resident, but losing her edge as she now was wheelchair bound. Last were the Vales, Todd and Joyce. Todd, the vice mayor, who actually was a good artist, was doing everything he could to avoid Mary Miller and her painting discussions. Joyce wasn't on the town council, but Charlotte had quite strongly suggested that she come—for reasons that no longer were valid.

From the way Joyce was angrily staring her down as the Vales entered the hall, Charlotte assumed that the owner of the B&B had, sometime during the day, learned what Charlotte already now knew.

"The equipment is all gone," Jason Williams announced to the gathered group as they sat down, not waiting for Charlotte to formally open the meeting. Charlotte didn't backtrack to recover the proper rules of procedure though. She knew that Mary had already written up the opening of the meeting before she got here. All meetings opened alike. Charlotte was particularly amused that her meetings supposedly opened with a pledge of allegiance to the flag, since the center's American flag had been missing since the last time the hall had been painted which was more than a decade before Charlotte had moved to Hopewell.

"No joke, Sherlock," Bonny Levitt answered to Jason's declaration that the construction equipment was gone. "We all can see that with our eyes. Them bulldozers are a little hard to miss."

Bonny wasn't known for her humor—just for her biting sarcasm. When someone suggested she might try doing something about that, she just answered that she'd survived three husbands, so she considered it was, as she called it, a realistic view of life that kept her alive. Out of her hearing others suggested that her attitude probably had been the reason for her husbands' early deaths.

"Yes, they are gone," Charlotte informed everyone—taking control of the meeting, or trying to. Hannah Helgerson took this moment to reminisce.

"I can remember when one of those big orange monsters was right here on Main Street," Hannah murmured in a sing-song voice. "They were putting in street lights. Of course all we've ever gotten of those were two blocks' worth, and most of them no longer work. But they had one of those large orange things with the arms—and there was a bulldozer too. No, maybe two. Boy did they make a noise. Sometime in '48 it was . . . no, now that I think of it—"

"Yes, well, the point is that the equipment that was clearing the point and the lot next to Brenda Boynton's is gone now," Charlotte said, overriding Hannah's soliloquy, no matter how fascinating anyone present was finding it—although Bonny Levitt had muttered, "It was 1950," which Charlotte chose to ignore.

"And they aren't coming back." Joyce Vale completed Charlotte's sentence, spitting words out like bullets. The stare she was giving Charlotte also recalled the word "bullets."

"Not coming back?" Don Dunkel said. He blushed then, realizing that he'd used a shocked tone. He had done his sympathetic best in commiserating with parishioners who wailed about the destructiveness of the machines in the town over the past two weeks. But, like more of the local merchants than just the Vales, seeing what was happening as an economic boost for the town, Dunkel had already ordered plans for the expansion of the Episcopal church building. He was grateful then when Jason Williams echoed his plaintive "Not coming back?" He'd already made a tidy little sum in doing on-the-spot repairs for two tractor engines.

Charlotte had found out the news earlier in the day when she called her Realtor, Scooter Wilson.

"I have learned that the Varios want the land because they are planning on putting in an unapproved gambling operation," Charlotte said to Scooter.

"Old news and over the hill, Charlotte," Scooter answered. "You really should have taken the offer when it was given. There's no way I'll be able to get that much from anyone else for your cottage, sugar." To Charlotte, the woman sounded like Charlotte's file had already been tucked away at the back of the Realtor's filing cabinet.

"What do you mean?"

"I mean that the Varios are cutting and running. The project is dead. Finito. And now they are clients of mine along with you. They want to sell it all off. Their project has become public—did you see the story in the *Baltimore Sun* this morning? You should send poisoned brownies to that reporter, Ron Rendel. He's cost you a bundle."

Charlotte bit her tongue. She'd almost said that she was the one who gave the story about what the Varios were trying to do here to Rendel and the *Sun*.

"It would have been an illegal operation, Scooter," Charlotte said. "It would have brought us all so much trouble that the money would not have been worth it. By the way, did you know what they wanted the land for?"

"For a resort, yes."

"Not for an illegal gambling casino? They kept you in the dark about that?"

"Look, Charlotte. There was a lot of money to be made off these deals—I don't have a responsibility to vet why someone wants to buy property that's for sale. You would have benefited greatly. And now it's all been blown up."

"Maybe not for everyone, Scooter. You handled the sales to the Varios . . . and now you are handling the sales by the Varios. So, you're coming out just fine in commissions coming and going, aren't you?"

The silence on the other end of the line was deafening.

"Anyway, I want to take my property off the market for now, and perhaps move it to another Realtor if I decide to sell." It wasn't that Charlotte needed the cottage—or still hoped she did—although Brenda's attitude about telling her son, Tony, about them made her think that it would be folly to give up a fallback residence. But the more she thought about the Gambling Commission appointment, the more she wanted to give it a shot. In view of this, it was probably a godsend she hadn't sold the place to the Varios—and now it would be good to distance herself from any hint that she might have done so.

"If you wish." Scooter's voice had turned to ice.

"And, Scooter," Charlotte had closed, "I think Brenda Boynton might want to have that lot next door to her house back. I trust you will settle on a good price for her if she does. I'm sure you realize how advantageous it would be to have Brenda on your good side."

"Yes, the project has been canceled," Charlotte announced to those gathered for the council meeting later than evening. "We are well shed of it, though," she continued, looking straight at Joyce Vale. "All of us are. The developers were gangsters, and they wanted to open illegal gambling operations here. This would have been a major headache for Hopewell and all of us. We might even have been involved in crimes ourselves—at least in a lot of uninvited police scrutiny of our lives."

"Like the deaths we're hearing about?" Jason said. "Does this all have anything to do with that graveyard they've found in the woods next to the Boynton house or that car they pulled out of the river off the point? I've heard that Anne and Bill Wells were in that car. Is that true?"

"Back in the late '50s and early '60s, it were, when there were lights and big black cars and all that mystery in those woods. Why, when I was a girl . . ."

Charlotte let Hannah drone quietly—in fact she now was sure that Hannah had provided very valuable information—but she raised her voice to respond to Jason. "Yes, we think Anne and Bill were in that car. The FBI is investigating. So, if any of you have heard from the Wellses in the past three weeks, please speak up; it will help the FBI from going on a wild goose chase."

Silence reigned momentarily as those gathered looked at each other for claims the Wellses were fine and having a ball in Mexico. Not hearing any such claim, Charlotte continued.

"They also are investigating the bodies buried in the woods next to the Boynton house. I'm sure we'll all be fully informed when those cases are resolved. And, yes, I wouldn't be surprised if that was all connected with this casino project and the gangsters involved in that. I think we all escaped a bullet here—all of us." She was returning Joyce Vale's piercing gaze.

"Yeah, right . . ." Joyce started to say.

"Yes, right, Joyce," Charlotte overrode her. "You can probably buy back those two lots your houses were on for a song now. And the buildings needed knocked down anyway. Someone else has borne the expense of that for you. You can build vacation houses there that folks working in Washington, D.C., will want to buy—or rent by the season. That's much better for your interests than you and Todd working with the Varios and maybe ending up like Anne and Bill Wells, isn't it?"

At that Joyce's demeanor was reduced to quietly sullen and Todd almost collapsed in shock. At least he had gotten the point, Charlotte thought. And no doubt by tomorrow morning he will have explained it all sufficiently to his wife.

"So, there's really no need for an extraordinary meeting of this council anymore," Charlotte said. "Yes, yes, Mary, I'd love to have a walk through with you on all of this . . . very colorful art. But, as I was saying, we can conclude the meeting and all go home. This will all get straightened out. I'm sure a few new vacation homes along River Street—or new resident retirees—will be a good thing for the town."

"I remember the Thompsons who originally owned that one cottage of Joyce's that got knocked down," Hannah was now relating in a low monotone. "Bank teller he was, that Mr. Thompson."

"Toms. Their name was Toms," Bonny interjected. "And it was her—Mrs. Toms—who t'was the bank teller. It's her who went to prison, not him."

"Never found all that money," Hannah was continuing on, as if she hadn't even heard Bonnie. "Some say it's buried under that house somewhere."

* * * *

"I'm glad I tracked you down. I thought you were staying with Brenda Boynton. I tried there first. No answer."

Sore point, Charlotte thought. But that's not what she said to Evan Worthington, the head agent of the Annapolis FBI office, who had reached her by telephone at the cottage. She too wondered why she wasn't at Brenda's house. Brenda hadn't called for two nights, just leaving Charlotte in limbo. Leaving Charlotte with all her insecurities on what was up with their relationship. Did having Tony home with her mean that Brenda was reassessing her relationship with Charlotte? Charlotte had no intention of competing with Tony for Brenda's attention and regard. Charlotte would just step aside if it came to that. It would rip her heart out, but perhaps it was best that she know it now rather than five years from now when there was nothing else in Charlotte's life but Brenda.

Charlotte nearly choked. There was nothing else in her life but Brenda now. Of course there were the dogs, Rocket and Sam. But they'd probably opt to go with Brenda too, given the choice. She nearly snorted at that thought. Charlotte was the one who usually fed and walked them—but it was Brenda's lap they put their muzzles in. Of course they were both male, and, Charlotte assumed in her self-deprecating way, that any male would chose Brenda over her. Hmm, she wondered. Would that extend to Evan too?

"Charlotte? Hello? You still there?"

"Yes, Evan, I'm still here. What do you know? Any sense coming out of all that has been happening in Hopewell yet?"

"Yes. There's light on the matter now, I think." There was a short pause of silence.

"And so?"

"And I'll tell you all about it over lunch—unless you have other plans. Say at the Hunter's Tavern in the Tidewater Inn in Easton? 1:00 p.m.? I'll meet you half way."

He'd meet her half way. That's one thing Charlotte would have to concede about Evan. He was willing to meet her half way. Was Brenda willing and able to do that in life now that she had her son back? And her movie career too? Brenda had come here—back to her home town—under a cloud, suspected of murder—and determined to retire. But that murder had been cleared up. Charlotte had helped clear that murder up. And now it looked like Brenda was increasingly being drawn back into the movies. Was there room for Charlotte between the movies and Brenda's son? Charlotte was a pretty hefty woman. She required a lot of room. Maybe Brenda was seeing her for what she was and was drawing away from her.

"That's blackmail, Evan," Charlotte said. "You could just tell me everything over the phone."

"I could, but then I'd lose the chance to have you all to myself for lunch. I'm not above blackmail to achieve that desired goal."

"Well, OK then, 1:00 at the Hunter's Tavern."

"You mean it? You give in just like that?"

"You know I'm too curious not to," Charlotte said, with a laugh.

When she'd hung up, she laughed again. But it was a hollow laugh. No, she didn't have any lunch plans. And anything was better than sitting around here in her cottage and worrying about what was happening up the street at Brenda's federal-style mansion—and obsessing over what it might mean for Charlotte's future.

Her greatest worry, though, was seeing Evan again when she was as vulnerable as she was now—vulnerable to his charms and to what he made no bones about wanting from her.

She looked up at the clock. Three hours. She had three hours to stew.

But then she didn't have three hours. The telephone rang again. It was Deputy Sheriff David Burch.

"David," she answered, with surprise. "I thought the FBI had taken over all of the investigations here."

"Not all, Ms. Charlotte. You asked that we search Clagett's farm real well, and I've had men out here doing that these past two days."

"And they are coming up empty and you need me to ask you to call them off? It's nice that you called, David, but it was just a suggestion. If you haven't found anything, that's fine. You can just—"

"It isn't that, Ms. Charlotte. We have found something. A body in the well. Medical examiner says it's a woman, a couple of weeks dead. I thought you might want to—"

"Edith Smith?" Charlotte asked.

"Sure could be," David answered.

"I'm on my way," Charlotte said, and she was, in fact, already standing and pulling a sweater on.

So much for sitting here and stewing for three hours, she thought. She should be shocked, she knew, but once again her finely tuned intuition had panned out. And once again she was on the hunt. Almost as if she'd never retired. Almost as if there was something in her life to propel her forward and to get her juices going other than Brenda Boynton. Or Evan Worthington, for that matter.

This time she'd need to take Sam and Rocket with her to Clagett's farm, though. She need to exercise them and let them do what dogs did if she was going to be in Easton for the afternoon.

* * * *

As she drove to Easton, Charlotte went over the strange case of the Smiths in her mind again. Two women, cousins, who were nearly identical in appearance. One was the reclusive, not-the-sharpest-knife-in-the-drawer, tacky-dressed widow who had taken up residence at a small, nonproducing farm just outside of Hopewell a couple of years earlier and was haunting the streets of the village and taking short-term, temporary domestic jobs. The other was a thief and a murderer who had made it onto the FBI's most-wanted list.

One of them, it appeared—or perhaps someone else altogether—had been in the well at Clagett's farm for the last couple of weeks. The medical examiner had said the dead woman had been strangled before she had been dumped in the well. The house at the farm had looked like a tornado had gone through it.

Was this the end of the hunt for Ida Smith—a hunt that Charlotte had conducted for nearly a year, fruitlessly, before she had retired from the Annapolis FBI office? Or was this just another notch on Ida Smith's belt.

Regardless, Charlotte would never feel fully retired until this case was closed.

As she drove, she half hoped that Evan would renew his offer for her to come back to the Annapolis office—to move back to the Maryland capital—and to consult for the bureau. This was the life she had been immersed in before retiring to Hopewell. Maybe this was the life she really wanted. And if she was going to be the chair of the state Gambling Commission, she could best do that from Annapolis.

One part of her hoped Evan would bring that offer back onto the table. It would break her heart for Brenda to tell her she didn't want her anymore. Maybe it would be slightly less tragic if it was Charlotte who made the break.

Evan got to the restaurant before Charlotte did and stood as she was escorted toward his table. He was wearing a big smile, and Charlotte marveled yet again on how handsome he was—on how well he had aged since they had been lovers back in Virginia.

"I can see the old sparkle in your eyes," he said as he pulled her chair out for her.

"It's the restaurant. Hunter's Tavern has always been one of my favorites."

"Then we must come here often," he said.

After they'd ordered their meal, Charlotte got right to the point. "It was dastardly of you to refuse to tell me over the telephone what you had discovered. Surely it's too soon for the lab results to be back on anything."

"Not if you are the chief of the office—and put an 'overnight' order on it. Then it only takes two days rather than the usual week or more."

"I was never able to get anything that fast," Charlotte said with a laugh.

"You were never the chief of the office," Evan countered. "But you could have been, you know. That's where you were headed when you up and retired."

Here it comes, Charlotte thought. He's going to ask me to come back as a consultant. Do I know what I'll answer?

"So, on the bodies in the car."

"Yes," Charlotte asked, letting her curiosity push aside her realization that she wanted Evan to ask her to come back to Annapolis and work with him.

"They were Anne and Bill Wells—the neighbors that you knew."

"Well, there's that then. I wonder—"

"But they also were other people—or at least the man was. We're still checking on the woman. His particulars match the laminated driver's license we found in his wallet in the car. He was posing as Bill Wells all right."

"But?"

"He was also someone else. Someone with a record from the sixties. His name at that time was Salvador Rizo. Does that ring a bell?"

"No . . . wait, yes it does. Wasn't Rizo the last name of whoever bought the wooded lot from Brenda Boynton's father?"

87

"Yes, it was. Clever girl. You remembered. You've still got the edge. The Rizos were a minor Mafia family from New York. As far as I know, Salvador was the last survivor."

Maybe this was where he would renew his offer.

"Beyond that I don't understand. Are you saying that after the Rizos bought the wooded lot, Salvador was installed here?"

"Yes, it looks that way."

"But to do what?"

"What have we found in the wooded lot?"

"Bodies. Lots of bodies."

"Yep. The Rizos were part of the Mafia wars in New York in the 1950s and the 1960s."

"Ah, that rings a bell. I've meant to tell you that when I interviewed Hannah Helgerson, our longest-lived resident in Hopewell, she said that the mystery of the wooded lot—at least until Brenda Boynton's mother's body was found there—concerned the night visitations the residents had seen. Big black cars and lights in the woods. Always at night."

"That figures. We're beginning to get matches on the bodies found there. It looks like that lot was a dumping ground for the Rizos' kills in their Mafia wars in New York. A couple of the bodies found have been identified as other gangsters who went missing in New York in the 1950s and 1960s."

"And Bill Wells? I mean Salvador Rizo? He was some sort of caretaker in residence—for the Rizos' dumping excursions?"

"It looks that way, yes. But the Rizos were on the losing end. So, when all of the New York Rizos were gone, it looks like Salvador

88

completely reinvented himself. And what better way to hide from the other families than to spend most of it abroad on archeological digs?"

"What changed, though? Why is he dead? And I assume Anne was just collateral damage?"

"I suspect we'll eventually connect her to the mobs too, but it doesn't matter in terms of the explanations we need. You ask what changed? The Varios arrived. That's what changed."

"That seems a bit of a coincidence, doesn't it? Two New York Mafia families mucking around in a quiet village in Maryland on the Choptank."

"That's what helped us unravel this. We have the purchase records on the lot. Brenda Boynton's father sold the lot to the Rizos. And when the Rizos were wiped out, The Varios took over the lot. Their interest in putting their casino resort here probably was grounded in already having land here."

"But the Varios hardly could have known about the bodies on the lot or have been involved in killing the Wellses here," Charlotte said. "Their worker uncovered the bodies on the lot and called the police—and it's their dredge that brought the Wellses' Toyota up. If they knew there were bodies here, they wouldn't hire contractors who unwittingly would uncover them. If they wanted to get rid of the bodies, they'd use their own people and pull them out at night—just the way they were put there in the first place."

"We think so too. And that's why we're not closing the books on this one yet. We believe that there must be some remnant of the Rizos still in existence and that they want to stay unknown. They probably went into shock when the Varios started digging around in Hopewell."

"And Salvador?"

"He probably was still in contact with them—the only link between them and Hopewell. So, suddenly Salvador became expendable. We've opened a case file on this. We have some Rizos to catch—if any still exist—and a lot of old New York mob hits to close."

Once more Charlotte thought Evan was building up to asking her to return—probably to work this case. But desert and coffee came and he hadn't said anything about it.

"I'm not sure why and how the Rizos ever acquired their killing ground here," Charlotte finally said.

"I'm afraid that gets laid on the doorstep of Brenda Boynton's father."

"Brenda's father?"

"Yes. He was a lawyer. He went from here to New York. And guess whose lawyer he was."

"The Rizo family's?"

"Bingo. There's no telling now whether he knew what they would use the land he sold them in Hopewell for. But we must assume he knew at least something about what was going on. His daughter said he was almost rabid about never selling or developing the land. There must be a reason he never told her the truth. And why he didn't tell her might mean that he knew what was under the ground there. Holding it as sacred ground because his wife had been murdered there might have just been a convenient blind for the real reason."

"Brenda will be devastated to learn that," Charlotte said, with dismay.

"There's no reason why she should ever know, Charlotte. That part of the case is long dead. No one need ever tell her."

"Thank you."

He turned serious then.

So, is this where he's going ask? Charlotte wondered.

"You think a lot of Brenda Boynton, don't you, Charlotte?"

"Yes, yes I do. I don't think I knew what life was before that. My husband—"

"I know you didn't have a good life with your husband, Charlotte. People in the office have talked about that. And I abandoned you too all those years ago."

"No, Evan, let's not go there. It was so many years ago. And there was Ruth. I was nothing compared to Ruth. And she wanted you so much."

"Please don't say that, Charlotte. Don't run yourself down. Ruth was a fine woman. But you are every bit as good as she was. It was all just bad timing."

"Yes, that's the story of my life. Bad timing."

"What I want to say, Charlotte . . . this is so hard for me . . . is that I completely understand why you feel as you do toward men . . . why you've. . . . Well, let's just say that I know that Brenda Boynton is a terrific woman. But if you ever. You know that I . . ."

As far as Charlotte could later remember, that was the end of the conversation. The waiter came with the bill at that point, they both awkwardly remembered that they were late getting to where they next needed to be—although Charlotte assumed that Evan didn't have an appointment he was missing any more than she did—and they found themselves out on the street, separating off to go to their separate cars.

On the way back to Hopewell Charlotte went over the conversation a hundred times in her mind—but she could never decide that Evan had actually asked her to do anything. Nor could she be sure what she would have answered if he had.

"What's the point of all of this?" she found herself saying out loud. But she didn't have an answer for that either.

Chapter Six: Coming Home to Good Fortune

Charlotte arrived back at the cottage to find her answering machine blinking, with a plaintive "Where are you? Are you upset with me?" message from Brenda. She called back immediately.

"I tried calling you earlier today, but there was no answer," Charlotte said as soon as Brenda picked up.

"DeeDee insisted on going shopping. I think we're much too rural for her here. We didn't satisfy her, I'm afraid. There were no haute couture shops within fifty miles of here."

"So did you buy anything stylish for yourself."

"No. All I bought were a couple of lottery tickets."

"Lottery tickets? I wouldn't think of you as someone who would buy lottery tickets."

"Oh, it's always been a little delight of mine—ever since I was a young girl and won a doll in a raffle at a children's movie. It's just been one of my little pleasures. I've been buying them weekly here since I moved back to Maryland."

"And have you won in other lotteries?"

"A few, yes. I guess you can say I've been lucky in life."

"I can see why you haven't said anything about it. People already envy you for your looks and talent and brains. If you add being lucky at gambling to it . . . but I guess there are limits to luck. If I wanted to be catty, I'd return to the topic of DeeDee and say you weren't all that lucky for Tony to be smitten with her."

"I'm not so sure that he's smitten as much as that she's convenient. He doesn't have to go outside of our little movie circle and bring someone in. She's conveniently here. It's probably the same from her end, plus her mother is pushing a romance angle with Tony for publicity purposes. But DeeDee obviously resents me. I think she was pouting that I was along for the ride. Sometimes with DeeDee you can't really tell pouting from just plain boredom. But they wouldn't have known even what way to turn on route 50 to find anything. DeeDee was such a pill over lunch that I sent them on to Ocean City to cope near the beach by themselves for the afternoon. They'll find practically nothing open there where DeeDee can shop in January, but she can window shop and they will be far more in the lap of the commercialism she's comfortable with there than here. I called Bea to come get me in Cambridge."

"Bea? Don't tell me."

"Yes, it's safe to come into my dining room again. I pitched Bea Helgerson just the way you told me to, and it worked a charm. When I told her about the separate suite in the basement and about the dogs' quarters down there, she was over here, suitcase in hand, almost before I could hang up the telephone. All she indicates she's disappointed with is that the dogs aren't in residence here. But I'm concerned why you haven't been here with us. I hope I haven't been the insensitive bumpkin and sent you away just because you aren't spending the nights here. And where were you for lunch? I called to try to entice you up here for lunch. Bea fixed some scrumptious shrimp salad."

"I went to Easton for lunch."

"By yourself?"

"No. I met a friend—from work. In Annapolis. We met half way." Charlotte didn't know why she didn't tell Brenda she'd met Evan Worthington for lunch. But she assumed there would always be a barrier there on that subject. "And I did rather get the impression that if you wanted me there while Tony and DeeDee were there, you'd let me know."

"Oh dear. I'm so sorry about that. Of course I want you here. Please come for supper. I promise I won't step into the kitchen even once."

"I could come now."

"Even better." What Charlotte wanted to say is that she could pack her bags and move back right now. Of course she couldn't do that. But just the knowledge that this was her first impulse told her that all of her speculation earlier in the day about what to do with her life from this point amounted to little. If Brenda beckoned, Charlotte would be there.

"Shall I bring Sam and Rocket?"

"If you don't, I'm afraid Bea will poison our dinner. She keeps asking me when I think the dogs might be back."

"Let's take our drinks to the library," Brenda said when Charlotte had arrived and Brenda was handing her a gin and tonic. "It's more intimate there."

Bea had immediately taken the dogs in the kitchen and had promised to put them down in their room after she'd had a visit with them and they'd gotten a snack.

"And we'll know when Tony and DeeDee are arriving back and have time to come out of our clinch," Charlotte answered Brenda's suggestion on locating in the library. She hesitated a moment before saying that, not wanting to poke the issue with a stick. But she couldn't resist, and she'd always been one to meet adversity straight on.

"Oh, do you think we'll be in a clinch?"

"I certainly hope so."

"So do I," Brenda answered in a small voice. "I've missed you terribly."

When they got to the library, with its inviting overstuffed soft-leather loveseat, there was a bit of the clinching going on. But eventually both got thirsty and, as if on shared cue, pulled away from each other and reached for their hi-ball glasses.

"I've been so busy walking on glass with Tony and DeeDee—well, almost entirely DeeDee—that I haven't had time to ask about what's going on with the investigation. I've noticed that the bulldozing has stopped next door. Are they still looking for bodies? Bea tells me that they've found several."

"Several" would be an understatement of the body count next door, Charlotte thought. She also thought this wasn't the time to talk about the Wellses' bodies having been found either—not unless Brenda brought it up herself.

"It turns out that down through the exchanges in property . . ." Charlotte didn't want to say how far down ". . . the land got into Mafia hands and they were using it as a mob hit burial ground. The Vario company that has been doing the demolition here wanted to build a clandestine gambling casino resort down on the point, on the land they bought from Win Engleton. They were going to do something with the wooded lot next door too. But with the publicity this Mafia burial ground will bring and the light that's been shed on the Varios' intentions for the land, they are pulling out of the project. They have Mafia connections too—but we haven't linked them yet to the gangsters who were using this for a burial ground."

"I wouldn't think they'd be digging in there if they'd known there were mob hit bodies there," Brenda said.

"Precisely. That's what the FBI and police think too. But what it means for you, Brenda, is that you probably can buy the land back from the Varios and leave it undeveloped again. The bulldozer hadn't made much leeway, it will wood up pretty quickly again, I think. So, if that's what you want—"

"It's something to think about. I don't think I want anything built there next door. So, maybe I will. It's probably silly of me to want to leave it vacant because of my own past memories."

"No, it's not, Brenda. Memories are important. So are relationships. I wonder—"

At that moment they heard the front door open across the house and Tony and DeeDee entering the living room next door.

"I hope that's enough shopping for you today," Tony said. "It's kind of funny that you tilted your nose up in all of those new-clothes boutiques we passed by but had a ball in that second-hand shop. I thought I'd never pull you out of there."

"Not that I was that anxious to come back here," DeeDee could be heard saying with that irritating little whine of hers. "Can we go back tonight to those clubs we saw on the hotel strip. We were recognized, so I think it won't be a problem in getting in. That would be fun. There hasn't been much fun here."

"Yeah, I guess we can. As long as you don't care that I won't drink much. It'll be a long drive back. And we aren't here just for the fun, you know, DeeDee. Brenda and I have had scripts to start memorizing."

"We could stay there tonight, couldn't we? It doesn't have to be all work."

Tony paused before he responded. Brenda started to say something in that pause to let the two younger actors know she and Charlotte were in the room just next door. They hadn't really had an opportunity to signal their presence yet. But Charlotte put a hand on her arm and, when Brenda looked at her, signaled that perhaps they should sneak out to the hall through another door and come back in to the living room via the front hall. They were standing up to do that, when DeeDee's next, cutting remark arrested their movement.

"Why do you hesitate? It's because you like having Brenda hanging on you isn't it? A woman nearly twice your age. Well, I don't have to compete with another woman old enough to be my mother for any man. This has been a fun ride, but—"

"There is no competition, DeeDee, and I'm tired of you flouncing around here like there is. Brenda's not interested in me. Brenda's in a relationship with Charlotte Diamond. Are you so self-absorbed that you didn't realize that?"

There was a stunned silence—and not just in the living room. In the library as well, where Brenda had taken on a shocked look that probably equaled what DeeDee was displaying in the living room. For her part, Charlotte had to turn away to keep from smiling. But she did so only briefly. She turned back to Brenda almost immediately and took her arm and led her out through the hall door and through the kitchen, where Bea looked up from her dinner preparation and smiled at them. Charlotte smiled back, asked if Bea could produce a couple of cups of tea, and led Brenda through another door and into the breakfast room which was as far away from the living room as they could go and still be on the main floor of the house. There she helped Brenda into a chair and then sat in the one beside her. Sam and Rocket padded out to the breakfast room, and the women let them stay, feeling the comfort they obviously were intent on providing by settling down on each side of Brenda's chair.

"I didn't think he knew," Brenda whispered.

"Apparently he does," Charlotte answered, resisting the urge to say that of course he knew. He'd probably known about Helga before Charlotte came along too. He'd probably come to an accommodation with that even before he knew he was Brenda's illegitimate son. "And apparently it doesn't matter to him," she added.

"No, it would seem it doesn't," Brenda said, still in that far-away shocked voice.

"So, what matters to you now?"

"Not that, certainly," Brenda answered, her voice stronger, a twinkle returning to her eye. "But it may mean that I'll have to ask Bea to make up the bed in one of the other bedrooms. I have a feeling that Tony and DeeDee may be in separate bedrooms tonight."

"And how do you feel about that?"

"As a mother? Fantastic. Tony's completely out of DeeDee's league, even if it's just the mother in me talking."

"It's not just the mother in you, Brenda. Tony indeed is a catch of the century."

"But there's something else too," Brenda said.

"What?"

"I think it's time you came home too. And there's no need for Bea to make up a separate bedroom for you. Screw DeeDee if that gives her heartburn."

"That's the spirit," Charlotte said. But she had a hard time getting the words out. What she wanted to do was to cry—to cry for joy.

After a gourmet dinner, during which DeeDee sat looking uncharacteristically pensive, and Brenda, Charlotte, and Tony chattered more comfortably than they had done for days, Tony and DeeDee did leave for an evening in Ocean City. Tony declared, however, that they would be back that evening—and he'd already requested the anticipated change in bedroom arrangements.

After they left, Charlotte left as well—promising not to be gone for long—so that she could pack up again and bring her things back to Brenda's house.

When she opened the door to the cottage, she saw that there were phone messages again. One was from the Realtor, Scooter, that Charlotte decided could wait—that the woman could dangling on the string for a while. Another message was from Deputy Sheriff David Burch, though, and he'd said she could call him back at any time, day or night. She called him back immediately, and he answered on the first ring.

She could hear that he was in a bar—and that there was a woman's voice in the background. But this didn't seem to inhibit him, so Charlotte didn't let it inhibit her either.

100

"I wanted you to know straightaway, Ms. Charlotte. We've caught up with her. She was in a woman's shelter in Baltimore."

"Ida Smith?"

"No, Edith. The body in the well has been identified as Ida."

Charlotte let out a deep breath of relief. It had been a long time coming—a very long time.

"Edith claims it was self-defense and that she then panicked and just pushed her cousin's body in the well and took off."

"That sounds like Edith on a normal day," Charlotte said.

"She says that she came home to find Ida rummaging through her house and that Ida had attacked her like a mad woman and that Edith was just protecting herself when Ida was killed. She's scared stiff, though, and is babbling most of the time."

"Is she in Baltimore or do you have her in the county jail?"

"She's in the county lockup."

"When you have a chance, could you go over there and assure her that her story is believable and that she shouldn't be in too much trouble other than for hiding the body and not reporting it. Tell her the FBI will back her up on the danger her cousin was. Oh, and tell her that Brenda Boynton and I will be by in the morning to see what we can do for her."

"Will do."

"And, David. Thanks. Thanks so much—for more than you can imagine."

When Charlotte disconnected, she sat down in the chair by the telephone and took a moment to let her breath regularize and her heart stop pounding. This was it. She was truly retired now. The Ida Smith case had been the only open one in Charlotte's case file on the day she'd

101

retired. It was never a big, important case. But she realized now that she hadn't come to closure on her FBI career until just this moment—when she heard the Ida Smith was no longer at large.

And with the lifting of that burden, Charlotte understood so much more about herself too. She'd had enough conflicting feelings about and for Evan Worthington and Brenda Boynton—and for the work she'd subconsciously believed she'd left unfinished. She'd probably never be completely over Evan, but that wouldn't matter. Not as long as she had Brenda.

In a week they'd be off to Florida—Brenda to film a movie and Charlotte to be a consultant for the movie. Not even the movie work or Florida mattered that much. The point—the only point that mattered—was that she'd be there with Brenda.

Charlotte looked around the living room of her cottage and suddenly it seemed so isolated, so lonely. It might be different if one or both of the dogs were here with her. But Sam and Rocket weren't here. They were up at Brenda's. That's where Charlotte knew she should be also. She struggled up from her chair and headed for the door.

She found Brenda slumped in a chair in her foyer, holding a letter—the envelope had fallen to the floor. The two dogs were sitting beside her and looking up into her face and wagging their tails. Brenda didn't seem to see them, and she didn't react to Charlotte coming through the front door either. She just sat there, looking dazed.

"What is it? What's wrong, Brenda?"

Brenda moved her mouth but she didn't seem able to speak. She lifted the hand holding the letter and waved it at Charlotte.

"What's wrong. Is it in that letter? Bad news?"

"Not exactly."

Charlotte took hold of the letter, but Brenda held it with such a tight grip that Charlotte had trouble wresting it away. Before she could lift it high enough to read, though, Brenda spoke again.

"It's the Maryland Lottery. I won."

"You said you won before. Did winning always have this effect on you?"

"I never won like this before."

Now Charlotte saw the letter, and her eyes zeroed in on the highlighted sum and she could barely speak and was looking around frantically for some place to sit down. She collapsed on the lower steps of the staircase leading to the second floor.

"Good god. This is for 98, Brenda. $98 million."

"I know." It was almost a wail. "What am I going to do?"

"The first thing we're going to do is to disconnect the telephone and get someone to filter your mail. And the next thing we're going to do is pack and thank God that we're off to Florida and that your filming plans haven't been made public."

Chapter Seven: En Route

"Well, here we are in an airport terminal again."

"I'm so sorry about the flight, Charlotte," Brenda said, putting her hand up to her head.

"Stop fiddling with that wig. Move it a micro inch and anyone watching you will know it's not your hair—and then they'll look closer and in no time your effort to disguise yourself will be completely blown."

"I'm sorry for that too. You must think I'm silly to want to travel in disguise."

"Don't be so sorry," Charlotte said, her smile belying the exasperated voice tone she was using. "I can quite understand why you decided to go incognito on this flight. Winning all that money in the lottery has naturally forced you underground to avoid the hounding public and all of their ideas on how you should spend $98 million. In your place I would have gone to a disguise a long time before this to stave off my adoring fans as well. That's not true, of course—you've had years to adjust to being adored by the public. I'd probably decide to go ahead and bask in it for a year or two. I haven't had adoring fans like you have."

"Oh, that's not true. You've had admirers of your detective work. I've seen the worship in their eyes. When the FBI came into the picture in the fiasco of that Ocean City casino we got mixed up in, I saw how much the agents respected you. And when the FBI chief agent Evan Worthington looked at you, I saw—"

"And don't apologize for the reseating," Charlotte interjected, not wanting to go anywhere near the subject of her old flame, Evan Worthington, in a discussion with her lover. "If we'd kept the first-class seats, the whole effort to go incognito would have been useless."

"You could have stayed in first class—with Tony and DeeDee. I could have managed in economy by myself. You didn't have to change your seat too."

"Where thou goest so goest I," Charlotte murmured. "Besides, the choice of sitting with you in economy or DeeDee in first class is a no brainer."

"I concede that point," Brenda said with her signature tinkling laugh. Charlotte realized in an instant that making Brenda laugh wasn't a good idea and placed a warning hand on Brenda's arm. A couple of the passengers sitting around them had looked up, startled when they'd heard Brenda's laugh, knowing that it was a familiar sound, but not quite able to place it as the screen laugh of one of their favorite senior movie actresses.

Charlotte gave Brenda a warning look, which was immediately interpreted correctly, and Brenda stifled her laughter.

To distract Brenda, Charlotte leaned in and said, "Can you tell me more about this movie we're going to Florida to film? What was the name of the original?"

"*White Orchid*," Brenda answered. "I imagine that's what this one will wind up being named too."

"Why the Everglades, and if Aaron Woolridge, the producer, told me much about why he wanted me to consult, that discussion was knocked out of my mind when he showed what they were willing to pay for my time and advice."

"The movies are rather a pleasant surprise in wages in comparison to government salaries, aren't they?" Brenda answered.

"Yes, and why the Everglades? For that matter, why is this a remake of an uncompleted film? We've kept too busy to discuss why you even were willing to do this film. When we left Hollywood, you were vowing that you were finished."

"It's mostly loyalty, I guess—why I agreed to do it," Brenda answered in subdued tones, "the same reason I went back to Hollywood for the last one." Both women hoped the discussion would be covered by the noise around them of restless people waiting for a delayed flight. Any discussion of a movie in the making was guaranteed to pique interest from anyone listening to the conversation.

"The movie was a special brainchild of the ensemble I've mostly worked with for years. It was one of our original projects, and both Aaron and Howard Holton, our director, had sunk considerable effort and some of their own money into the movie plan. It's from so long ago that it was one of those Vietnam War films taking advantage of patriotism and an renewed interest a decade later in the veterans of that war who had been ignored—or, worse, blamed for losing the war—

during and immediately after that war. War films lifting up soldiers were popular in the eighties. The film was actually a clever idea, I thought. It was about a film crew filming a Vietnam War movie. We went to the Everglades to replicate the marshy, jungle locale of Vietnam. David Runion and I were both cast in it. We'll both take smaller, older roles now. Tony has been hired for David's role."

"And DeeDee for your original role?"

"Maybe, maybe not. I'm not sure that Aaron and Howard see DeeDee as a younger me, and they may have had the roles and actors imprinted in their minds too long to be comfortable straying too far from the original types."

"I certainly hope neither of them see DeeDee in you. The quicker Tony ditches her, the better for all of us, I think."

"Oh, I think their liaison is mainly promotional. It certainly is from DeeDee's mother's perspective. But I suspect there is some of that from Tony as well. It's no different from how everyone paired David Runion and me all those years—and laughingly, it turned out that he preferred men and I preferred women."

"I certainly won't complain about that," Charlotte responded and then took Brenda's hand and squeezed it, which was the limit of the affection she felt safe to show in these crowd-swirling conditions. "But why me as a consultant? I don't know a thing about Vietnam—or the Everglades, for that matter. Am I just being thrown candy to keep you happy on the set?"

Brenda looked startled and then she snorted, causing a couple of the people around them to look over. When they'd lost interest, Charlotte said. "Because, if that's how I'm supposed to consult, I'm all for it."

Brenda started to laugh, but Charlotte squeezed her hand hard, which stifled the danger of those nearby hearing Brenda's signature laugh.

"No, it's because of the reason the film never was completed. White Orchid wasn't a flower or a 'thing.' That was the name of the main character of the movie—of the lead of the movie within a movie. White Orchid was a young, half-Vietnamese, half-European woman—although I think the actress cast was really half Chinese. Aaron has said that the audiences wouldn't be able to tell the difference. However, not too far into the filming she disappeared."

"Disappeared?"

"Yes, foul play was suspected. They never found any trace of her. And they suspected all of us at one time of doing her in—we were not a particularly happy crew and there was even a lot of sexual tension. For some reason the FBI got involved as well. I'm not sure the actress was properly documented and there was some hint of her being a foreign agent. David once asked if Europe extended to Communist East Europe—in connection with the actress's origin—and all he got was a dirty look from Aaron."

"The FBI?" Charlotte mulled this for a few minutes, then she asked, "Was John Lu, who did many of the scripts for your ensemble movies, the scriptwriter on this too?"

"Yes he was. In fact he was the one who wrote and pitched the project notes for the movie."

"Hmm," was all Charlotte said out loud, but her mind was spinning on possible connections. It was highly unusual for the FBI to be called in on such matters. But recently, only a few months ago, while they had been in Hollywood, John Lu had been revealed to have been a

Chinese spy who operated on the East Coast under the name of Edward Chang. Charlotte had seen his FBI file and had recognized him in Hollywood, blithely working under another name in the movies—in a role in which he rarely would be photographed and publicized. If John Lu was engaged in spying in connection with this film on the Vietnam War and that had anything to do with the disappearance of the main actress, maybe Charlotte could understand why it would be a good idea for her to be involved in this remake—and maybe, at the same time, to do some delving into that young actress's disappearance over thirty years ago.

"So, I guess Aaron thought it would be good to have an FBI consultant on the movie—if only for publicity purposes. He's indicated that he and Howard might be able to use the mystique of the earlier filming somehow both in the new movie and in the publicity for it. Does that make sense?"

"Yes, of course it does," Charlotte answered. And now, for the first time, she actually was interested in having a role in the making of this movie. And also, her concern for the safety of Brenda was heightened.

This increase in a need to protect Brenda prompted Charlotte to look around the waiting lounge, instinctively using the surveillance skills she had honed during nearly thirty years with the FBI, looking for any source of recognition of who would be on the flight from Baltimore to Miami in disguise. Brenda was traveling incognito partly because the studio wanted the filming of *White Orchid* to be done completely in secret. They wanted it to get a splash of publicity, of course, but only after it was finished and done with a gasp of "Brenda Brandon has returned to the movies" when everyone was saying that she had retired for good. Brenda's lottery win only made a disguise even more convenient.

So intent was Charlotte on scrutinizing the crowd that she almost didn't hear Brenda.

"Again, I'm sorry that me traveling in secret has caused the change from first class to economy. I know how much you dread the confines of the seating in that section."

"It's only a three-hour flight," Charlotte said. "Nothing like our flight from Amsterdam after the Rhine Christmas cruise was. I surely can manage . . . oh damn."

She had stopped in mid sentence. Brenda looked up in alarm. "I haven't been—?"

"No, I don't think you've been recognized. But I recognize someone. I hoped to have left my investigative life in the past, but it seems to be following me around."

"Excuse me? What have you seen?"

"It's who I've seen. Dexter Reardon, if I'm not mistaken. And I've seen his mug shot often enough to be quite sure it's him."

"Dexter who?"

"Reardon. He's a major gangster. Murder, extortion, kidnapping, gun running, drug dealing. You name it, he's involved in it."

"And he isn't in prison?"

"We've never been able to catch up with him. I'll have to go make a call, Brenda. The FBI will, I'm sure, be interested in knowing he's on his way to Miami. There's a lot of trouble he can get into in Miami."

She started to rise and then sat right back down. "I think he's seen us and recognized one of us."

"One of us? Why not just you?"

"He's known to be an obsessive movie buff. I wouldn't be at all surprised to learn that he had a crush on you."

"Wonderful."

"No, don't look at him. He's looking over at someone and motioning in our direction, drawing the man's attention to us. It looks like another goon. It figures that Reardon wouldn't be traveling alone. Hold tight for a few minutes. Wait. Good. They're calling the first-class passengers for boarding, and he and the other goon are headed for the gate. So are Tony and DeeDee. They're doing well; they haven't looked over at us once that I can tell."

"It's all just a day on the set for them, Charlotte. I gave them a script to follow, and they are doing as they are trained to do."

Charlotte stood up. "I've got to go make that call. Sorry."

Brenda started to laugh again, but then she clamped her hand over her mouth—but only for a few seconds. When she pulled it away, she was smiling. "With you there's no such thing as uneventful travel, is there?"

"I had hoped this would be the start of an entirely new life," Charlotte answered.

"Fat chance of that," Brenda countered. "We're on our way to a movie set, darling. There will be nothing normal or uneventful there, I can assure you of that."

"And not in between, either, it would seem," Charlotte muttered when she was well away from Brenda's hearing.

* * * *

Brenda and Charlotte were greeted by the service crew at the airplane end of the gangway, as they entered the American Airlines Boeing 738 that would take them nonstop from BWI to Miami International. In Miami someone from the movie company would meet them for the trip across the tip of Florida on Alligator Alley to Naples and down to Marco Island. First was a perky and cute "Hello, my name is Chip" steward of trim but diminutive stature and spiked blond hair. He was seconded by a chorus of two "Welcome aboard" stewardesses, one a brunette and the other a red head, both perfect Barbies, who identified themselves as Ginger and Rachel.

Upon running this gauntlet, with Brenda turning her head away with the assumption, upon Charlotte's prompting earlier, that the air crew would know she was aboard and would be looking for her, Brenda and Charlotte spilled into the first-class cabin, where the passengers were already seated.

"Won't there be other celebrities aboard?" Brenda had asked.

"Trust me," Charlotte had replied, "you'd be the one they'd zero in on unless there are a couple of rock stars on the flight as well. You are the flavor of the week. It isn't every day that a movie actress wins a lottery with almost $100 million in jackpot money."

Here Charlotte truly felt like she was running a gauntlet en route to the economy class section. There were sixteen first-class seats, rows 1 through 4, two seats each on either side of the aisle. Tony and DeeDee were in seats 2A and 2B. Both looking away from Charlotte and Brenda as had been worked out beforehand. Immediately in front of the cabin door, in 1B, was the goon Charlotte had spied in the waiting lounge. The 1A seat was vacant. Cattycorner to him, back in 4C, with 4D vacant, was the gangster, Dexter Reardon. The seats Brenda

112

and Charlotte had given up, 2C and 2D, were occupied by a pair of high fashion runway models, the older of which Brenda had recognized back in the waiting lounge and pointed out to Charlotte. The woman in 2C was Samantha Gaines, who, with age, had progressed to being an announcer at international fashion shows and who Charlotte had first remarked on to Brenda because she looked so much like Brenda.

An elderly couple occupied 4A and 4B. Two middle-aged businessmen, already pounding away on laptops, were sitting in 1C and 1D. 3A and 3B were empty. But it was the man who was seated in 3D who arrested Charlotte's attention. She recognized him immediately, and she could see that he at least thought he recognized her too, although he didn't do more than look surprised at seeing her. It was Clifford Stainer, the U.S. Justice Department's chief legal counsel. He had been dictating a letter to a young man in a navy blue pinstripe suit sitting next to him in 3C with a laptop computer on his folded-down tray.

Charlotte had a brief moment of panic as she shifted her bulk back and forth down the aisle toward economy class at the thought that Dexter Reardon might be on the flight to do harm to Clifford Stainer, and her mind was already churning over how she might be able to take Stainer aside to warn him. Reardon was sitting right behind Stainer. That didn't seem likely to have been an accident.

There wasn't much she could do about it now, however. She was being pushed along by the tide moving down the long aisle in coach class, wondering if this plane even had a seat 29F. Unfortunately it did, just three rows in front of the tail of the plane, with its service galley and two bathrooms.

Unfortunately too, the plane was nearly fully booked. Brenda and Charlotte had changed their seats to 29D and 29F with the assurance that 29E would be left free. But the booking agent lied.

"I'm sorry. I think my seat is the one at the window," Charlotte said, trying her best to smile through the dismay of seeing in seat 29E a Hispanic woman almost as big as she was with an assortment of shopping bags that spilled over from her lap onto the seat Charlotte was supposed to be in.

The woman just looked up at Charlotte like she was a wild woman.

"29F, the window seat," Charlotte repeated, slower and louder. She held out her boarding pass so the woman could see the seat number on it.

Initial noncomprehension, upon which Brenda whispered in Charlotte's ear, "This probably isn't a good idea. There seem to be two empty seats in first class. We could switch back."

"Not a good idea either," Charlotte whispered back. "You have a plan, remember? It's just three hours. I'll manage, thanks."

By now, the large Hispanic woman had gotten the idea of what Charlotte was trying to tell her, and with mutterings in Spanish that Charlotte didn't want to be translated, the woman was unwedging herself from her seat and stumbling out into the aisle. A smiling Rachel appeared as if by magic and began divesting the complaining woman of her shopping bags and finding places in the overhead up and down the aisle to stash them.

Still, when Charlotte managed to contort her way into her seat, she found that shopping bags were stuffed under the seat in front of her—as well as under the woman's seat next to her. She looked up to

114

say something to the stewardess, but smiling Rachel was already floating back up the aisle toward first class. And anything Charlotte could have said anyway was choked off by the air that puffed out of her when the almost-as-large-as-herself Hispanic woman landed back in the middle seat and pushed Charlotte's body up against the window.

Charlotte turned toward her, smiled weakly, and said, "You can have the window seat, if you like. I'm happy to switch." At least then, Charlotte, thought, she'd be able to sit next to Brenda. They had much to discuss, including, if Brenda had recovered enough from the shock to discuss it, what Brenda was going to do with $98 million more on top of her existing fortune as well as the abandoned construction mess they'd left home in Hopewell on the Choptank. As town mayor, Charlotte had had quite a few problems land in her lap, but she and Brenda had issues to resolve themselves, like whether Brenda was going to buy back the half-wooded lot beside her house that she had thought she already owned but didn't and whether Charlotte should try to sell her riverside cottage and move in with Brenda permanently.

Without a word in response—and very likely not having any idea what Charlotte had offered—the woman wedged between Charlotte and Brenda gave Charlotte a venomous look and snapped open the satchel on her lap, took out a foil-wrapped burger she'd apparently bought in the terminal, noisily opened the wrappings, and chomped down hard on the burger. Mayonnaise squirted out the side Charlotte was on; she didn't even want to think about where that had gone.

Charlotte looked across her to where Brenda, eyes twinkling, was doing her best not to laugh.

At that point Charlotte realized she hadn't eaten lunch herself and the plane wouldn't land in Miami until 6:00 p.m.—and, worse, that she hadn't visited the restroom before boarding. The call she had to make to the FBI on the presence of Dexter Reardon on the flight had made her forget.

Three hours. Only a three-hour flight. She was already regretting that word "only."

* * * *

Charlotte didn't even realize that she had dozed off after takeoff when she was nudged—or more like jabbed—awake by the elbow of the Hispanic woman applied sharply to her side. She almost jabbed back before she was awake enough to realize where she was and who had nudged her—and calculated who would probably win a elbow-jabbing fight in these confines.

The voice that accompanied the jostling, though, was male. And it was remotely familiar.

"Charlotte? You are Charlotte Diamond, aren't you?" the voice was saying, cutting through the fog of her drowsiness.

She turned her head toward the aisle and opened her eyes—and she winced in pain, having developed a crick in her neck from the position it had taken against the inside edge of her window in the plane's fuselage.

"Charlotte, this man is asking for you." Charlotte instantly recognized this voice. It was Brenda's voice, and it sounded slightly concerned. She was suddenly alert.

"Clifford Stainer. Yes, we've met."

116

"I'm sorry to disturb you, but could you come forward—to the first-class section? I think we may have a situation requiring your skills."

"My skills? My FBI skills?" Charlotte still wasn't all there. If she had been, she wouldn't have blurted that out. It abruptly ended conversations and turned heads in the rows immediately adjacent to theirs. The Hispanic woman's eyes went round as saucers, and she noisily sucked air. Charlotte also noticed that the woman's toe pushed the bag underneath the seat in front of her deeper into the recess. Charlotte's mind clicked into an "I wonder what's in that bag she doesn't want me to know about" speculative thought, but she shook head with the self-admonishment that this wasn't her concern.

She couldn't see how there would be any problem up front that should be her concern either.

But then Brenda muttered, "Tony?" and Charlotte overrode this by starting to stand.

"OK, Cliff, I'll come with you if there's any chance I can get out of where I'm wedged."

Brenda was up immediately, concerned but also half shocked that she had indicated a connection with anyone in the first-class section. And the Hispanic woman was also struggling up from her seat, seemingly looking for some way to make herself invisible—something that, if difficult for the zaftig Charlotte, would be quite impossible for the rotund Hispanic woman. Brenda moved out into the aisle to start the process of unwedging Charlotte.

Stainer leaned in toward Charlotte when she'd struggled out of the row and into the aisle.

"Disappearance of a passenger," he murmured.

"On an airplane?" she responded, perhaps a little too loud.

117

"Let's go up front," Stainer said, and then he turned and started moving forward. Charlotte followed him, already clicking her mind into gear, after she turned and whispered to Brenda.

"If it has anything to do with Tony, I'll let you know right away."

Charlotte's training was to observe everything, so she didn't wait until she got to the first-class section to start investigating. She moved her head back and forth and walked slowly, taking in everything she could see. Stainer, quite far up the aisle already, turned and grimaced at Charlotte. But almost immediately he realized that she was looking at everyone, assessing and checking. He nodded his head slightly and then turned and moved to the closed curtain between the classes.

Many of the passengers were dozing—or trying to—or were withdrawn into themselves in the limited space provided in economy and trying just not to be there for the three-hour flight. Those who were paired off were leaning in toward each other and absorbed in talking in low tones. However, the farther Charlotte moved forward the less that this was the case and the more alert and agitated the passengers were.

Charlotte knew why this was so. There were sounds of wailing, in a female's voice, coming from the first-class section. It was obvious that someone up there was having some sort of fit.

The retired FBI agent's homing-device attention went to a man, maybe in his early forties, strongly muscled, with a bullet head and crew cut in the 14C aisle seat. He looked to be professional military, and he was on alert the same way that the people—both criminal and law enforcement—would be in Charlotte's career life. She could tell he was tense and ready to spring at any moment. He was the most interesting of the people she'd seen on her walk forward—in terms of a disappearance

118

issue—and his seat number lodged in her brain. She'd ask for a manifest as soon as she had assessed the situation so she could start checking him out.

The situation Charlotte found when entering the first-class section put the need to bring order to the world first on her list. One of the models—the younger of the two—who she'd seen sitting in the fourth row on what was now to the right of the aisle from Charlotte's approach was in hysterics.

"They've taken her. They said they would and it's done. My god, somebody help us!" the woman was crying out.

The flight attendants were fluttering around the woman ineffectually. Charlotte reached through and took the young, skeletal form by the arms and shook her hard, taking all of the wind out of her sails and not calming her down completely, but starting to neutralize her tantrum.

"Do you know if there is a doctor on board?" Charlotte asked of one of the stewardesses.

"Yes, there's one right here."

Charlotte saw that the elderly man she'd seen on her earlier pass through the section had risen from across the aisle and had opened the overhead bin above his seat. He was reaching for a bag. The bag that he brought out was almost identical to the one under the seat in front of his.

"Anything that will pass for a tranquillizer in that bag?" Charlotte asked.

"Yes, I think so."

"Let's see if we can get this young lady quieted down."

First crisis on the way to being controlled, Charlotte thought. But she hadn't missed the young model's plaintive rant about a threat to Samantha Gaines, the internationally acclaimed supermodel of two decades earlier. And the first-class section wasn't so large that, in looking around quickly, Charlotte couldn't clearly see that there was no Samantha Gaines there.

Well, this is something new, she thought right before she kicked into doing what she'd been well trained to do.

* * * *

"Excuse me, what's your name and that of the missing woman?" Charlotte asked the young model as the woman sank into her airplane seat under the increasing influence of the sedative the doctor had given her. It wasn't the first thing Charlotte wanted to do—she really wanted to launch an immediate search of the plane—but this young woman might pass out from the sedative before she could answer questions, so Charlotte needed to pin her down on what she knew first.

"I'm Bianca."

"Bianca what?" Charlotte answered. "Please, everyone, back off a bit. She needs air." The steward and the doctor were crowding into the row where Bianca was huddled. Charlotte looked up to say something to the steward, but the doctor was the first one she saw. She did a double take at not seeing who she expected, but then she frowned and let the thought that then raced through her mind retreat, pushed aside by concern for the young model.

It seemed like everyone in first class and the steward and the stewardess named Rachel, the other one—Ginger—having gone with

120

Clifford Stainer—after he'd flashed his FBI credentials—into the pilot's cabin to explain what was happening in the passenger compartment and to establish contact with authorities on the ground. All but the doctor and the steward, Chip, backed away, but the buzz from their talk was still fairly loud.

"Just Bianca."

Charlotte cursed the world of modeling under her breath but focused back on the young woman, who was babbling on now. "We were going back to Rome after Miami. I told her it wasn't a good idea, but she said she wasn't afraid, that she wouldn't let it control her life."

"Who is she and what was she afraid of? Your seatmate? Is that Samantha Gaines?"

"No, it's not, it's the movie actress, Bren—," Chip started to say, but Bianca was surging ahead.

"Yes, the international model, Samantha Gaines. We are on our way to Miami for a runway assignment, but then I wanted us to go back to New York. But Samantha said no, we'd go home to Rome. That she wasn't scared."

"No. The manifest says this seat is occupied by—"

"The manifest's wrong," Charlotte turned to Chip and said. He was holding a clipboard in his hands, which Charlotte took to have the flight manifest on it. "Someone else should be in this seat, but tickets were changed. I know, because I was supposed to be sitting in this seat that Bianca's in."

"This isn't the seat for Bren—?" Chip asked in shock.

"No, it's not." Charlotte turned back to Bianca, who appeared to be starting to drift off under the influence of the drug. "Stay with us a

121

minute, Bianca. What kind of threat are you saying Samantha Gaines is under?"

"Kidnapping. It's rampant in Italy, but connected to New York too. The police in New York told her that she's on a list of celebrities that gangs are trying to kidnap. Not just for the money. For the publicity too. And now they've done it."

Charlotte straightened up and her eyes went to the gangster Dexter Reardon, who—along with the goon sitting up front—seemed to be the only first-class passengers not all aflutter over what was happening.

"You, young man, you're with Clifford Stainer?" Charlotte barked.

"Me?" the man who had been sitting next to Stainer and taking dictation from him when Charlotte passed them upon boarding answered. He had been standing in the aisle just down from where Charlotte and the doctor and Chip were huddling over Bianca. "Yes, ma'am. I'm with the Bureau too. Doug Meyer. Can I help?"

"Yes, could you go back and sit beside that gentleman in the back row of first class, please? He's Dexter Reardon, a person of interest to the Bureau. He may be able to help us with this inquiry."

"I don't think—"

"Just do it, please," Charlotte said. "I know Cliff Stainer has told you I have his authority."

The young agent didn't look happy about this assignment, but he turned and started back to where Reardon was sitting.

"As for you, steward and stewardess," Charlotte said after she'd sent the agent off. "Chip and Rachel is it? And you two." She was indicating the businessmen who had been sitting in 1C and 1D. "And you, doctor, and your wife too—and that young gentleman over there"—here she was indicating Tony Trice but trying not to reveal that she knew him—"Could you start conducting a thorough search again—I know a search has been done—but a very thorough one now. A woman can't just disappear on a closed-fuselage flight in the air. If she's on—"

Charlotte didn't have time to finish that thought, as Dexter Reardon reared up in his seat in the face of the approaching FBI agent—as, across the first-class compartment—the goon in the first row did as well, and all hell broke out.

At that same moment, the figure of a strongly built man barreled through the curtains from the economy-class compartment, pushing Doug Meyer into Dexter Reardon and causing those two to tumble back into the seats in row 4, brushed between Charlotte and the doctor and the steward and stewardess as well, and careened into the body of the goon in the front row. An arm was raised, the hand holding a plastic gun that almost looked like a toy, and for a split second all held their breath, waiting for the shot that could pierce the skin of the plane and depressurize the cabin.

Doug Meyer was back up on his feet quickly, though, and stumbling toward the front of the cabin.

Charlotte shot a hand out and grabbed hold of the arm of his suit jacket. "No, wait," she cried out. "Stay with Reardon."

* * * *

Clifford Stainer, emerging from the pilot's cabin with the stewardess, Ginger, right behind him, assessed the situation instantly, moved two steps to his left, and reached up and took the gun out of the goon's raised hand. The younger agent pulled the goon's arms down and pulled them behind his back. Stainer reached into his jacket pocket, pulled plastic cuffs out, and snapped them on the goon's wrist. Doug Meyer, who had ignored Charlotte's command and rushed forward, then pushed the goon back in his seat with the comment, "Sit there and be a good boy now."

He stood back up and started to round on the man who had rushed up from economy and who now was calmly standing beside the door into the cockpit. Meyer went into a crouch, ready to spring at the man. Clifford Stainer also was squaring off on the interloper.

"No need for that, Cliff," Charlotte called up to them. "And please can come back here now and sit with the man I asked you to watch. We can ask the air marshal to watch that gentleman for us."

"An air marshal?" Stainer said. He also, though, was giving Charlotte a pointed look that made her start to reassess the situation.

"Yes, I spotted him as I was coming forward. I figured him either for an air marshal or a criminal. I'm glad I guessed correctly. But is there something—?"

Stainer gave Charlotte another warning look and then turned away from her. "Don't worry, we won't damage Mr. Reardon," Stainer leaned down and said to the goon, who was hunched down in his seat and glowering. "We just want to talk to him for a few minutes about the disappearance of this woman." Then Stainer came down the aisle to Charlotte, pulled her away from the doctor and the steward, turning her so that they couldn't see or hear what he said to her. Doug Meyer continued on to the back of the section and sat across the aisle from Dexter Reardon.

"This is fortuitous for me, Charlotte, but we have to be careful. May I let you proceed on your investigation and I'll interrogate Mr. Reardon for you. I'm quite sure he's not involved in this disappearance. He's going to Miami in secret arrangement with us. We were going to have a little chat on this flight, with his associates being none the wiser. But the wrong bodyguard has accompanied him. We thought we'd lost the opportunity, but now we have another one—that is if the bodyguard up there doesn't wise up to what we're doing."

"I understand," Charlotte said. She swiveled and said to those gathered, who mostly were still recovering from the now-neutralized threat of the waving gun, "Mr. Stainer and his associate are going to speak with this gentleman. Could the rest of you who are willing, fan out across the airplane and see if you can find the missing woman. You've all seen what she looks like, I think."

"Ms. Diamond? Did the FBI gentleman call you Ms. Diamond?" It was the steward asking the question.

"Yes."

"So you are the one who moved from this seat?"

"Yes."

"Back to . . . ?"

"Nearly all the way back to Baltimore, if you must know. Now, please, can you all go search for this woman? Not you, though, doctor. Could you monitor Bianca here? She seems to have passed out now."

The searchers scattered—Tony; the two businessmen; the doctor's wife; the stewardess, Rachel; and the steward, Chip, back into the economy section, and the stewardess, Ginger, up to the cockpit to report to the pilots. DeeDee wasn't asked to help in any way, and she didn't offer. She sat, reading movie magazines, as chaos revolved around her. Charlotte didn't object; that's how she wanted DeeDee—out of the way. Doug Meyer sat in the seat next to the goon in the first row to make sure he stayed put and didn't try to intervene in Stainer's little discussion with the gangster, Dexter Reardon, on topics that included providing names and rundowns on activities and turning states evidence.

Charlotte was moving back toward the pair to ask Reardon a few questions. Based on the reason he was there, she saw no need to consider that he was involved in the woman's disappearance, but to survive in his business, he must be especially observant. His seat was at the rear of the section. So, she wanted to ask him about what he might have seen.

She had almost reached the two men, when all three of them looked up in shock at the sound of a high-pitched scream.

Ginger was standing just outside the door to the cockpit, facing the forward galley kitchen, and pointing in that direction with an outstretched hand. Doug Meyer and the doctor were the first to reach the galley. By the time Gretchen reached them, they were lifting an unconscious woman off the floor of the galley.

"The missing Samantha Gaines, I presume," Charlotte said, as she approached.

"Yes, it's the woman who was sitting next to the other model, I'm sure," Doug answered.

"But she wasn't here before," Ginger said in a strangled voice.

The woman was unconscious and her clothes were rumpled in a way that no international model would be seen dead in—unless, of course, that's how the style of the moment had been designed to look.

"Get her over to this seat and lay her down," Charlotte said. "And, doctor, could you examine her, please?" The woman looked as knocked out as Bianca now. Charlotte wasn't all that surprised, though.

By this time, most of the searchers from the economy cabin were returning to first class, drawn by the scream they'd heard. Rachel stayed at the curtain between the classes, preventing the curious from economy from coming forward.

Charlotte walked to the front of the plane, signaling for Ginger to join her, and they went into the galley for several moments. When they emerged, Charlotte walked swiftly back down the aisle, ignoring the questions and comments that the others were pelting her with. She reached the curtain between classes just as the steward, Chip, was entering from economy.

Grabbing him by the arm, she declared in a commanding voice, "Come with me."

"Excuse me?" the steward said.

Ignoring him, Charlotte swiveled and said, "You too, Mr. Meyer, if you please. And bring that gun you confiscated from the bodyguard—unless you have one of your own."

"I do," he answered.

It looked more formidable that the plastic-shielded one the goon had managed to smuggle on board, so Charlotte opted for him to carry that one at the ready.

The three stumbled down the aisle, Charlotte again ignoring the stares, comments, and questions directed her way by the confused and frightened passengers in economy. She was virtually manhandling Chip, who was half her size, down the aisle, with Doug Meyer following in their wake.

127

When they got to row 29, Charlotte held Chip in place and growled at him, "Where is she? What have you done with Brenda Brandon?"

Chip's mouth was moving, but nothing but a squeak came out.

"Never mind, I know," Charlotte barked. "Mr. Meyer, hold this man here, please. And not too nicely if he tries to move off—although there's really no place for him to go."

The Hispanic woman was looking up at the three of them with fear and confusion written across her face. But she was the only one sitting in that bank of three seats. Brenda no longer was there.

Charlotte hurried to the galley at the back of economy class, where she searched for the button Ginger had shown her in the forward galley. Pushing it, she heard the whir of a mechanism, and the under-the-counter laundry hamper made the return trip up the elevator shaft from the lower deck.

Charlotte carefully and tenderly lifted an unconscious Brenda Boynton from the hamper and hugged her close to her. The beating of the heart against her was strong and reassuring, and Charlotte took a moment to compose herself before she left the galley, carrying the unconscious actress with a physical ability she'd later marvel that she had managed, and returned to row 29 where, while giving Chip a dirty look, she spoke to Doug Meyer.

"Do you have any of those plastic cuffs like Clifford put on that hoodlum in the forward cabin?" she asked. And when Meyer acknowledged he did and took a pair out of his pocket and, at Charlotte's direction, pulled Chip's arms behind his back and locked up his wrists, she said, "Do you have two more pair?"

"I have one more—Mr. Stainer probably has another pair too," Meyer answered.

"Good. We'll probably need two."

They marched back up the aisle toward the first-class section, Charlotte refusing any help with carrying Brenda. When they reached the first-class section, Charlotte laid Brenda in the free row of seats.

"Would you like me—?" the elderly doctor said, as he moved toward that row.

"Don't . . . you dare come near her," Charlotte said. "How long are these sedatives supposed to last?"

"I don't understand?"

"I suspect you understand perfectly," Charlotte said. It came out almost as a hiss. "I should have suspected when I turned around earlier, expecting to see the steward but seeing you instead. Doug, could you cuff the doctor here too—and perhaps his wife over there? She is the steward's mother, isn't she, doctor? Because you are most definitely his father—I could see it in your faces; if my mind hadn't been racing on other matters, I would have called you on it earlier. And this little kidnapping spree involves all three of you, does it not?—using the laundry chutes to send the victim to the lower level. It wasn't Samantha Gaines you wanted to kidnap; it was Brenda Brandon. But you were screwed up because the manifest wasn't updated. You took the model to be the movie star. When Chip realized the mistake, he tried to pull a switch, bringing Samantha Gaines back up and then going back and luring Brenda Brandon to the aft galley. But by then the crime was revealed. Meanwhile, the doctor here was sedating everyone in sight. I ask again, doctor. How long will these women be out?"

129

* * * *

"We were fortunate that they had so little time to set it up and were clumsy about it," Charlotte explained to Brenda in low tones, as she held her companion close. They were sitting in the seats they had originally been assigned—which had figured in most of the confusion of what had happened. Brenda had regained consciousness within a half hour, as had the international model, Samantha Gaines, who was being soothed in similar fashion in seats A and B of the 4th row. Tony and DeeDee had been moved to the first row, in front of Brenda and Charlotte, and Chip and his parents and the bound bodyguard were sitting in the A and B seats of rows 1 and 2, with Clifford Stainer, Doug Meyer, and the air marshal circling around them with "don't you dare" looks and pistols in their pockets.

The gangster the FBI was so interested in, Dexter Reardon, was sitting in the 4D window seat where he had started. Stainer was dutifully ignoring him, but the few hours on the ground during which the bodyguard would be processed for having a loaded gun on an airplane and attempted assault before the gang's lawyers could be brought into play would give Stainer and Reardon plenty of time to secretly discuss the state's evidence Reardon was expected to provide. Someone else would have to investigate how the bodyguard was able to get a hand gun—even a plastic shelled one—on the airplane in the first place.

They were only a half hour out of Miami, and the plane was already on its descent. Brenda looked out of the window at the fast-approaching ground and shivered. Then she turned back toward Charlotte.

"So, it was the steward and his doctor father who set this up—to get at me for my lottery winnings."

"That was the prize, yes," Charlotte answered. "But it was all the mother's idea. And the landing crew in Miami is being interrogated even now. They would have required help to get you out of the laundry basket and past the security checkpoints. I have a feeling that the mother is the brains of the outfit and that if they'd had more time to work on it, they might have had a good plan. Chip had seen your name on a preliminary manifest and mentioned it to his parents, who were aware of who you were and what you had just won. I guess the opportunity and greed to make a quick killing overcame their scruples and a sense of what the risks and problems involved were. Still, if we hadn't changed our seat booking without Chip knowing about it, it might have worked. He lured Samantha Gaines to the forward galley, thinking she was you, where his father was waiting with a knock-out syringe. When Samantha went down, they dumped her in the laundry basket and sent her down to the lower level. Accomplices in the ground crew in Miami would take you from there.

"When Chip found out from me that he'd gotten the wrong woman, he jumped at the chance to be part of the team searching economy class. He found you and, using a syringe his father had given him, he and his mother repeated their scheme in the aft galley. By then I was on to him, though. I could kick myself for not having identified the strong family resemblance between the steward and his father earlier."

"You were quicker to catch on than anyone else would have been," Brenda said. "That FBI official has been singing your praises. What I can't understand is why they would kidnap me if they wanted my money. What was the point of that? Who would be able to release my

131

money if I wasn't available to do so—and what would make them think I had the money in hand this quickly? Why didn't they kidnap you instead and make me pay for your release? I would have done it in a instant."

"As for the last question, I'm too big to fit in one of those laundry bins."

They both had a good laugh at that, and Charlotte was very pleased to hear the signature tinkling laugh from her lover. This meant that, indeed, Brenda wasn't the worse for wear for the experience. Charlotte racked up resilience to the list of Brenda's many talents.

"No, they wouldn't have had any idea who I was and what we mean to each other. And, no, they weren't thinking it through very well. It was an impromptu opportunity, and they weren't thinking clearly."

Brenda became pensive and turned her face back to the window, as objects on the ground became more distinct and the plane, which had been flying out to sea, parallel to the coast, banked slightly and came across the shoreline.

"I had a dream—no, more of a vision—while I was drugged."

She was speaking so quietly that Charlotte had to lean into her and listen carefully for what Brenda was saying.

"Yes?"

"I had a large group of my friends gathered around me—yes, you were there too Charlotte. Most of those I could identify, though, were people from the past in the entertainment world—in movies. All aspects of the movies, not just on stage. You know, some say that the movie world is a cutthroat one, but I didn't find it as such. Yes, there are one or two evil, grasping people. But I'm sure there are those in all walks of life. For the most part people in the movies were very kind to me."

"That's so, I'm sure, because you were always kind to others. The doctor said you would have some strange dreams while you were sedated."

"They weren't strange. It was more like everyone was looking at me, expectantly, wanting something from me but too polite and having too much regard for me to ask."

"Well, you'll find that's not the case with people coming to you for handouts from your lottery win." Charlotte almost snorted when she said that.

"That's the point, I think, Charlotte. I have all of this money I don't really need. And I've had a wonderful career—and have known so many wonderful people. You know, Charlotte, I think I know what to do with the lottery money—if you don't object. And we can make it pubic enough so that those who might beg me for a handout will know that it's all already committed."

"Why would I object? It's your money. I have everything I need too—even beyond you, which is all I really need. Do what you want with the money."

"I keep thinking about all that clearing the construction company did on the point in Hopewell, everything down from your cottage. The damage is done, but . . . and so, I thought maybe I'd just buy up all the land and develop and endow a retirement community for movie folks. Many of them want to stay around Los Angeles, to remain close to the industry—and nearly all of the retirement communities are located there. But some are made sad about no longer being in movies, and to them, living near Hollywood is a constant heartache. And so few of them have thought ahead and retired with enough money to live on. The image of the rich movie star holds for so few. I'd like to give them a community to live in where they won't have to pay much but will be well taken care of. What do you think of that idea?"

"I think that's a splendid idea, Brenda. I'd be happy to help you make that a reality."

The plane was leveling off, approaching the runway, and the seatbelt sign blinked on. Brenda instinctively reached for the purse that had been brought up from coach class and extracted a compact out of it and snapped it open.

"Oh, my god, I look terrible," she exclaimed as she saw her reflection in the compact's mirror.

"You could never look terrible," Charlotte retorted. "Just put on some lipstick and a smile and you'll have the world at your feet."

"And my wig. I've lost that. I'll have to go back and see if I can find it."

They were on the ground, at the gate, and the engines had shut down. The sound that predominated was passengers flipping open their cell phones and frantically texting or jabbering into them.

"What's the point? I think it's too late for the wig," Charlotte said. "I think you'll find the reporters three deep in the reception lounge by the time we get there. I just hope someone will be here to whisk us off."

There indeed, were reporters and an official reception party waiting for Brenda and Charlotte—well, mostly Brenda. They were permitted, along with Tony and DeeDee, to deplane early, but the prisoners and the air marshal and FBI agents—and the gangster Dexter

Reardon—had already been removed from the plane, which gave the media the time and opportunity to gather.

A beaming movie producer, Aaron Woolridge, and a more concerned-looking lead actor, David Runion, were there to retrieve Brenda and those accompanying her. This wasn't how Woolridge had seen the buildup of publicity for this film going, but he was delighted with how it was forming up. Of course he hadn't been the one to be knocked out and dumped down a laundry chute.

Olivia Stowe

Olivia Stowe is a published author under different names and in other dimensions of fiction and nonfiction and lives quietly in a university town with an indulgent spouse.

Other Books by Olivia Stowe

The Charlotte Diamond mystery series
- By The Howling
- Retired with Prejudice
- Coast to Coast
- An Inconvenient Death
- What's The Point?
White orchid Found

The Savannah Series
- Chatham Square
- Savannah Time

Inspirational Christmas collections
- Spirit of Christmas 2010
- Christmas Seconds 2011